99 MILES FROM L.A.

P. David Ebersole

99 Miles From L.A. by P. David Ebersole

ISBN: 978-1-949790-58-0 (pbk)
ISBN: 978-1-949790-60-3 (hbk)
ISBN: 978-1-949790-59-7 (ebook)
ISBN: 978-1-949790-63-4 (audio)

Cover design: P. David Ebersole
Layout and book design by Mark Givens
Author photo by Anthony-Masterson

First Pelekinesis Printing 2022

For information:
Pelekinesis, 112 Harvard Ave #65, Claremont, CA 91711 USA

99 Miles From L.A.
Lyric by Hal David, Music by Albert Hammond
Copyright © 1975 EMI April Music Inc. and Casa David
All Rights for EMI April Music Inc. Administered by Sony Music Publishing (US) LLC,
    424 Church Street, Suite 1200, Nashville, TN 37219
International Copyright Secured All Rights Reserved
Reprinted by Permission of Hal Leonard LLC

"Dover Beach" by Matthew Arnold, 1851, Public Domain.
"Time" by Percy Bysshe Shelley, 1824, Public Domain.
"Because I could not stop for Death" by Emily Dickinson, 1880s, Public Domain

Library of Congress Cataloging-in-Publication Data

Names: Ebersole, P. David, 1964- author.
Title: 99 miles from L.A. / P. David Ebersole.
Other titles: Ninety-nine miles from L.A.
Description: Claremont, CA : Pelekinesis, [2022] | Summary: "A hard-boiled crime story with a bi-sexual love triangle peppered with double-crosses. A music professor, an unhappily married woman, and a Mexican bartender band together to steal a buried fortune"-- Provided by publisher.
Identifiers: LCCN 2021046555 (print) | LCCN 2021046556 (ebook) | ISBN 9781949790580 (paperback) | ISBN 9781949790603 (hardback) | ISBN 9781949790597 (ebook)
Subjects: LCGFT: Detective and mystery fiction. | Bisexual fiction. | Novels.
Classification: LCC PS3605.B4665 A615 2022 (print) | LCC PS3605.B4665 (ebook) | DDC 813/.6--dc23/eng/20211005
LC record available at https://lccn.loc.gov/2021046555
LC ebook record available at https://lccn.loc.gov/2021046556

www.pelekinesis.com

99 MILES FROM L.A.

P. David Ebersole

Keeping my eyes on the road I see you,
Keeping my hands on the wheel I hold you,
Ninety-nine miles from L.A.
I kiss you, I miss you,
Please be there.

Passing a white sandy beach we're sailing,
Turning the radio on we're dancing,
Ninety-nine miles from L.A.
I want you, I need you,
Please be there.

The windshield is covered with rain, I'm crying,
Pressing my foot on the gas, I'm flying.
Counting the telephone poles, I phone you,
Reading the signs on the road, I write you,
Ninety-nine miles from L.A.
We're laughing, we're loving,
Please be there.

ONE

He sings along when he drives. His voice won him awards when he was young and it's far from unpleasant now, but he learned long ago that no one was going to pay him to be a professional musician in life. Still, he loves to sing. He holds the notes on the vowels because that's the way to sound good. You can't hold a consonant. In the car he always tries to imagine an audience because it makes a difference. You sing better.

The oncoming traffic becomes the blinding foot lights in his mind's eye, the rain on the windshield stands in for that faint murmur of the crowd, the wet tires are cocktails being served. Even though you can't see the people, you look straight ahead and you sing, outward, at all of them and to each one of them, simultaneously.

He had those dreams, yes, but he has had a lot of dreams that did not come true. This current one, though, this one's going to work. Because it isn't a dream, it's a plan. And this is the very last part of it now. Everything else worked. All the three of them have to do is come together, keep their heads, and not fight.

He's pretty sure she's gonna be mad she was hit so hard, but it had to be done to make it look real.

Ramon though, Ramon will be glad to see him, he's damn sure of that. If he's there. He said he'd be there.

"Ninety-nine miles from L.A..." He hums the words he doesn't know.

She also could get mad because he was already planning how to see Ramon without her being there. Anyway, she doesn't know about him and Ramon, so she can't be mad. Even if she is, who cares. He's spent his whole life trying to please people. No more.

He was supposed to drive to the desert tonight. Ramon'll be out there too, but not at her Palm Springs house. They can't risk that one of them has been followed. But who would follow them for a hundred miles without picking one of them up? If the cops were on to them, they'd've stopped the car by now. And if her husband somehow figured it all out, he'd be dead before he hit the 111.

"Ninety-nine miles from L.A..."

You know why the movie stars all went to Palm Springs back in the day? According to local lore, they were salaried and under contract to the studios who wouldn't let them go further than 100 miles beyond the Studio Zone when they were engaged on a film, so they could be called back to set.

The Studio Zone started in the 1920s as a six mile radius from Rossmore and 5th street and slowly elbowed its way into a thirty-mile circle emanating out from La Cienega and Beverly. Literally, a circle on the map, drawn as if there were a compass anchored at that street corner. To this day, anything inside the circle is fair game to ask actors to come to set for filming without paying them for travel. Once upon a time, the scuttlebutt was that it also dictated how far they could stray on their down time. The furthest thing out west, just outside of the thirty-mile Studio Zone, is the Forest Lawn cemetery in Covina. And 99 miles from there? Palm Springs. Well, really you were still inside of the 100 all the way to Rancho Mirage, which is why some say so many of the Frank Sinatras and Bob Hopes had houses out there.

In time, it came to be known as the "two-hour" rule, but that's likely a modern interpretation because before the 10 freeway was installed circa 1965, it would have taken a good three-plus hours to get from Los Angeles to the celebrity playground that was The Desert Inn. There's an oft repeated rumor that the real reason the likes of Rock Hudson and Jayne Mansfield skipped out of Hollywood to spend weekends in this little sin city had more to do with "morals" clauses in their deals that restricted them from engaging in various and nefarious activities, and so getting that far out of town unofficially meant they were off duty. Even the gossip columnists let their hair down and joined the party.

He read all of this history right after she told him

Palm Springs would be their getaway town.

Another weird fact: did you know you can't make someone testify if they live 100 miles away from the location of the trial? It's called Rule 45. A subpoena can only command compliance within 100 miles of where a person resides, is employed, or regularly transacts business in person.

That's neither here nor there, though, since her husband would never let this thing end up in any kind of court.

Funny when you're driving and you're thinking and a song comes on and it's got all the right lyrics. Well, almost right. He always thought the song was about being ninety-nine miles up the coast, driving towards L.A. and of course right now he's driving the other way.

If you skip the middle verse, the lyrics could be about going ninety-nine miles *away* from L.A. But there's no place that you would see a white sandy beach as you drive to Palm Springs. He thinks on that for a second. It could be that you live in Malibu somewhere off of the Pacific Coast Highway, so to get out of L.A. you would be driving south towards the 10 East, and the first thing you see as you are pulling out, off to your right, is the white sandy beach, which sparks the first memory, and so then you are turning the radio on and fantasizing about this place that is ninety-nine miles *from* Los Angeles.

Because, yeah, all of his dreams now were wrapped up in being far away from that godforsaken shithole, not going towards it.

He shook his head and slapped himself. Driving alone at night is always hard. You get mesmerized by the dark void. That's why he likes to sing. It puts your mind on something else. The meaning of the lyrics. The sound of your voice. How you would sing it versus the rendition you're listening to. How you could make it a hit. Maybe it should be the first song on your record. Or maybe it should be buried, a deep track and they discover it.

He hit replay so he could sing it again. He knew the cadences a little better so he was sure to do a better job this time.

The live Johnny Mathis version is really the only version. Art Garfunkel's is muddy, and Dionne's a goddess but her rendition of this one came late in her career so it's comparatively over-produced. Albert Hammond wrote it so you'd think his was the definitive recording, and he had the #1 Adult Contemporary chart topper. But hits don't mean a thing when it comes to judging quality—not in music, not in movies, not in art.

Hammond's also the guy who penned and performed "It Never Rains in Southern California" which everyone thinks is an anthem about how pretty it is in the land of fruits and nuts, when really it's about how crushing it is to dream of fame and success, and that's the problem with Hammond's singing. His writing, devastating. His voice? It lets you off the hook, you ignore the tragedy, remember the catchy part and forget there's a whole goddamn song behind it. You can blame the audience, but that's the singer's responsibility. On second thought, maybe that's Hammond's genius. If you can make people sing happily along to your words that are damning their whole existence, well, that's quite a trick.

Anyway, the point is when Mathis sings it, you see it. His hands are on the wheel. The rain is on the windshield, like tonight. It's there.

He'd gotten ahead of the song, though, because the intro is long and there was nothing to imagine yet, but that's normal when you're a singer. When you're a singer, the intro is the part where you have to feel what's coming. You don't just sit there, waiting for your first note. You picture the whole thing. You see it all laid out before you, like how he could see this whole deal right now, coming together the way it was planned.

What she'd say is that he could have found a way to apologize if he wanted to. But he knew not to get caught by that, he knew the answer to that trap. He was playing it safe. He was sticking to the plan. Which is ironic considering what he had already decided to do on arrival.

TWO

The way they met was sad. He liked to walk through the UCLA sculpture garden when he was in between classes or academic responsibilities. An adjunct professor of vocal coaching and music performance, his students admired him and he'd often find one of them hanging out, maybe under the Rodin. *Le Homme Qui Marche.* Or leaning up against Zuniga's *Desnudo Reclining.*

A self-described bi-sexual, he always felt this next admission marked him as cliché but he'd tell any one of them who asked that he liked the Henry Moore the best, the one called *Two Reclining Figures.* If he was going to picture himself inside any one of these sculptures, he'd tell them, he'd join the party on that one. That usually got a laugh and at least a raised eyebrow out of either sex he was talking to.

He vowed: never sleep with a student. Too easy of a mark and too depressing to think about why they want to be with you. It's unethical, he would tell himself. But lunch conversation was ok, even if it got a little flirty.

This particular day he was in a mood and he didn't care if he did something he shouldn't. He'd just walked up the hill from Schoenberg Hall, after suffering through the professorial version of a prisoner going up for parole: Academic Review. Imagine sitting silently before a group of yahoos who hold your future in their hands. A gaggle of losers you wouldn't talk to at a party, much less listen to their opinion on how you should conduct yourself. You know the type, with dandruff and bad suits. And those are the women.

These days the whole thing is made worse by a common practice that should never have been allowed in the first place: student evaluations. Not evaluations of the students, mind you. Written evaluations of the professors, by the often disgruntled and now fully empowered undergraduates. Towards the end of the term, some impartial emissary from administration interrupts your class, unannounced, and tells you to leave the room while they pass out forms that encourage "constructive criticism" of the instructor and the course itself. Imagine paying customers (the students actually refer to themselves as such) leaving Yelp reviews all the while knowing they are about to get a B instead of an A for their lackluster performance and middling talent that deserved no higher than a C minus, at best.

No one questioned his popularity with the students but, in Academic Review, the good notices get summarized and the bad ones get read aloud to you. After a couple of niceties, the Board of Yahoos who know nothing about you other than your name and the classes you teach tear in. "Often rude," they call you, based no doubt on a remark from that idiotic kid who always sat in the front and interrupted you to say he knew better so, yeah, you told him to shut up, and yes, often. "Can be dismissive," they remind you, likely because you told that oversexed and frankly brain dead sorority girl you would not meet her for a coffee or a drink to explain what you meant when you said she has no tone. "I don't know if I learned much," lobbed a non-committal ne'er-do-well with whom he would likely agree. "One day he literally seemed bored," said more than one student, and he can tell you the exact day they are talking about because he wasn't bored, he was hardening into stone— witnessing the whole lot of them miss their cues like they were in a high school choral group, trans- forming him into some inert soldier who didn't know he shouldn't look at the hideousness that is Medusa.

At the end of this warfare against your humanity, the Board agrees you can continue teaching but you need to improve your attitude if you are to be recom- mended for a more permanent and better paying position, and then they ask if you have anything to say in your defense. To argue against the commentary at the end of the review only adds a little tick next to a box with the word "insubordinate" or causes one of your esteemed peers to scribble "seemed defensive," so what you do is swallow hard, smile, say thank you for the feedback and leave. And die inside just a little more.

Being a teacher is demoralizing. Helping other people become what you never were able to do. Maybe that's a bad way to look at it, but after a while it gets to you. It pays like crap and when you're an adjunct you get no benefits. And since a class gets broken out into weeks, you feel the calendar. You look at them and you can see who you used to be and now you know: Like most of them, you're never going to be anything. You're never going to have anything, either.

So on this particular day, he was feeling so low he was considering quitting. On this particular day, he would've robbed a bank if you asked him to, and who'd ever think how close to that he was about to get.

When he sidled up to her, careful, apologetic for the disruption, she was crying over her pitbull, Daisy, who was clearly so sick it couldn't move. She had been to the vet already and they told her it was too late for any more surgery, the cancer had metastasized, but she couldn't bring herself to pull the trigger, so to speak. She grabbed the mutt up, wrapped it in this blanket she had in her trunk and decided to have one last moment with the old girl, outside, under some trees, in nature. Poetic, huh?

But a lousy sappy verse, more Rod McKuen than John Keats. The Romantics. They knew how to spin melancholy. That thought would have started her crying again if he hadn't asked if she was a student, which made her smile, thinking there's no way he thinks she's young enough to be enrolled here. She took it as the first sign that he had come over with some idea of picking up on her.

She went to school at UCLA twenty years ago, starting late, when she was twenty, as an English major which is such a joke, she said, because what the fuck are you supposed to do in life with an English Lit degree? Anyway, that's how she knew about the sculpture garden. And poetry. And how romanticism relates to death. And then she quoted a poem she knew by heart:

Because I could not

stop for Death,

He kindly stopped for me

The Carriage held but

just Ourselves

And Immortality.

Well, to be fair, she explained, Emily Dickinson wasn't a Romantic. She was a Realist. But her brand of realism romanticized death, and that's about as romantic as you can get.

Trying to relate and banter on her level, he recounted that the only poem he knew by heart was "Dover Beach" by Matthew Arnold. He had to memorize it in class when he was an undergraduate. He was pretty sure his teacher called Arnold the first true modernist, even though he wrote that ditty way back in 1860-whatever, and by modern he meant it was a damning account of humanity, from what he could remember, with the whole confused alarms and ignorant clashes by night et al.

Unable to focus, she turned his voice off as he spoke and, deflating, sunk lower down, putting her cheek over the still warm belly of the dog.

Realizing he'd lost her, he sat down to put a sympathetic hand on her back and when that caused her to let out that uncontrollable sob, to his surprise, he cried with her for a moment and she liked that. He struggled for some comforting words but she was the one who said there really was nothing to say. It was over. Or it would be, the minute she decided she had done justice to this poetic gesture.

But now she had a problem. All this grief and crying had taken it out of her. She was not sure she could carry the dog back to her car by herself. She barely got it here. The parking lot they put her in is pretty far down the hill. She asked for P3 but it was sold out so they put her in P2, way down below the Herb Alpert music building.

She had an idea if he'd go for it, which is that she could go get the car if he'd stay there with her dog, but of course, he stopped her from going any further with all of that. The music building is where he works so he offered to walk with her and do the carrying. That's where she really broke down, at the car. What was he to do, let her drive in that condition?

He called his coordinator and said to tape a sign on the door for the students: Class Cancelled, Family Emergency.

And so he drove her Rolls to the vet.

He held her hand when the doctor put the needle in and she clung hard and close against his chest, sobbing again after she saw that awful last breath pass out of the yellow-toothed muzzle of the "only real friend I've ever had." That's how she described that cancer-mangled gray-faced skinny junkyard mongrel and it pretty much ripped his heart out right then and there.

She needed a drink and she knew where she wanted to go.

THREE

Ramon was her bartender on many a dark day so they were friendly, but he could hardly be called a friend, she told him. She parked her car in the alley and drank here alone, because it was away from everything. No random neighbor or one of her husband's employees would see her.

That was the first she mentioned of her marriage, but words can be said with so much bitterness that you know more than you should right away. Her version of "husband" rang with a whole history of unpleasantness underneath it. She had decided she couldn't go back home once the dog was gone.

The house represented so many awful and disturbing choices she'd made in life. It had gotten lonely, hating him, and hating herself so much. Too lonely. With the dog beside her she could see her way out of it every day to make do with the mess she'd created, but now...

She trailed off and apologized for being so blue. He said he was interested and so she told him some more. Ramon caught his eye and gave him a look. He'd heard the whole yarn before. More than once. And he could tell you, the story gets drearier the more Manhattans he serves her. But he served her however many she wanted. Why wouldn't he? She ran a weekly tab and paid her bill without fail, in cash, and tipped 100% or $100, whichever was larger.

She liked Manhattans because they sounded writerly. Drinking them made her feel like she was at the Algonquin at a round table instead of at the corner edge of the bar of this skanky Culver City haunt. The Cinema Bar. Ha! The name made her snigger, especially when some screenwriter wannabes wandered in thinking it was going to be something cool. It was fun to banter with them because she could run circles around their dumb asses, but then she'd get bored. She was so far from any Hollywood anything, though, by desire and by design, she knew she was safe in here. The bulk of customers Ramon had to serve during the day were alcoholics with nowhere to go who liked the price tag of a $4 healthy pour for bottom shelf well liquor.

A standard 750ml bottle of booze has 16 regular shots in it. Let's say it costs the bar $10 for that fifth of, say, bourbon. If you keep it to a shot per drink, you make $64, or a $54 profit. Even if every drink you serve has a double shot, the house is still making a three hundred percent mark-up. This is why Ramon's boss told him not to worry about the pour. And Ramon wasn't stupid, he could do the math himself: you own the building, you're paying an undocumented worker in tips only who is lucky to have his job, so you're raking it in even if all you sell is rot. The minute some fool points at the top shelf stuff, that's where the profits run up. For the boss. Still, even knowing all of that and even if his numbers were all wrong, Ramon didn't steal from the bar: (a) he needed this job and (b) when you make the customer happy, it leads to higher tips. It's all small potatoes, but hey, it pays the rent.

Anyway, just after Manhattan number two, she confessed to marrying her easy-on-the-eyes mean bastard of a husband for money because she was broke (and still pretty enough to do that) and because it sounded like a better idea at the time before she had to live with it. And after this many years, how could she even get an apartment if she tried to start over—though being homeless probably couldn't be that much worse.

She excused herself and stood up to go to the bathroom. Before she did, she leaned over and half-drunk stage-whispered that she couldn't go home tonight. She's got ideas about something really big if anyone would listen but she'd have to be able to trust the person.

On that one, Ramon gave him another, longer look. Ramon was one of those undeniable beauties where you wonder how they ever could have ended up "here." Why didn't someone make him a model or a spokesperson or a goddamn Marlboro Man?

Because life is cruel, that's why. No one ever saw Ramon's grey-green eyes against that caramel brown skin and decided they could make a buck off him. Maybe he's not even legal. So far he hasn't said a word so who even knows if he speaks English. If he does, he's got a thick accent, too thick to get a real job in the land of plenty that ends up being a trap for so many of so many backgrounds, origins, and ethnicities. So here he stands, pouring bottom shelf booze to day drinkers and no doubt living in an apartment with a TV smaller and older than the one over the bar.

Ramon could feel when a man was watching him, much more than when women did, so he introduced himself and stuck out his hand, which meant he was asking the obligatory first question. Frank, he told him. His own name always sounded made up anyway, so he liked using a fake one if he didn't think he'd ever see someone again.

Ramon wanted to know how "Frank" knew Shelley and he quickly recounted the day's events, leaving out the part about his working as a teacher at the University. Strangers shouldn't know that much about you and Ramon didn't ask any further questions. Yet.

Ramon nodded silently when he heard the story about coming straight here from the vet because he knew then it was gonna be a *mala noche*. He told Frank to be careful about her tonight because he could tell when she was going to end up too drunk to get home, and this was likely headed towards the worst. She loved that dog and since she pretty much never went anywhere without her, Ramon got to like her too. He begged her to get the dog one of those fake vests that make people think it's a service animal so he wouldn't get in trouble with his boss, or worse, the department of health, but Shelley lied. She said she tried and the dog refused to wear it. Even Ramon had to laugh at that one.

Anyway, there's a hotel around the corner where she keeps an account and she can get there in a taxi if Frank doesn't want to be responsible. The hotel knows to call Manny, her husband, so he doesn't call out his goons. Ramon didn't want Frank to think she was a bad person. He deals in bad people a lot and she isn't one of them, he said. Her heart's been broken but it's good. Bartender philosophy at best, but with that accent and with those eyes, it sounded like the truth.

He would learn later how much Ramon really knew about Shelley, after the plan started to really fall apart.

FOUR

The cannabis business sits on the ledge between being a normal, above-board operation and a wild west renegade club owned and operated by outlaws. The problem for those running what should be a legitimate endeavor is that federal law does not accept the state's classification of it as an authorized enterprise. Banks in the United States are federally owned and operated, so, long story short, it's best to avoid opening an account with your cannabis money.

That means no checks, and no credit transactions.

He couldn't wrap his head around it so Shelley put it more simply. The whole she-bang tends to get done in cash. Your customers pay in cash, you pay your employees and suppliers in cash, your payroll, sales and income taxes — all cash. And no armored car companies will help you transport any of it because guess what? They are also contracted with the federal government.

At this point, Frank and Shelley had been seeing each other for a month, secretively of course, and it was true that she always paid for everything with sawbucks, Jacksons and Benjamins. Half the time it smelled faintly of dirt and she explained it was because her husband made her bury it. They had so much of it they had to have a map of their yard, like pirates, to know where it was. Have you ever seen five plus million dollars in small bills? It takes up a lot of real estate. And what was in the garden was not even the half of it. That was just the money Manny was skimming off the top without claiming it. Dirty money, literally.

He thought about it for a minute while he looked at her, naked in his bed. They only saw each other here now, in his little furnished apartment, in the bad part of Hollywood, down by the police station off of Franklin. Not even the foothills. She wasn't drinking as much and her looks were coming back. She was always a handsome girl, with bold features, strong eyes, messy-chic Monica Vitti hair and even a similar big-lipped reluctant smile, but the booze made her face puffy. That first day he thought it was because she had been crying so much, but the stories Ramon told him when he went back into the bar looking for her, to see her again and to tell her he quit his teaching job, made him realize she had more to drink over than that dog. He went in every day for a week and that's how the affair with Ramon started. An empty bar in the middle of the day means the employee can shut and lock the door if he wants to. Apparently Ramon wanted to.

The first sign that Frank was in over his head was that he was making the daily brutal trek from

Wilcox to Sepulveda that he swore he'd never do again the second he quit UCLA. It's scarcely 12 miles but with lousy traffic, it can take longer than ninety-plus minutes. Why? Traffic. Everyone knows the quip by Bette Davis about her advice to a young actress about the fastest way to get into Hollywood: Fountain Avenue. Ms. Davis died, though, long before greedy developers did whatever they've done to this city-spinning-over, building "live, work, shop, play" environments skyward, ad infinitum, with zero regard for population flow. Fountain won't do anymore. You have to zigzag up, down, and sideways to circumvent street closings and clusterfuck clogs, like a soldier on a battle mission in an uncharted forest. Imagine being a minimum wage worker having to do that drive, dodging around $100,000 leased SUVs manned by trust fund millennials staring blankly over their smart phones into the abyss, with airpods in their ears, making left turns (without signaling) in spots where Delongpre thins to one lane.

Listening but not listening, Ramon would nod at him as he stood by the door, describing what he'd been through to get to him, all the while closing in closer, turning the lock behind his back, and quieting him with a first kiss.

When she finally did show up that next Wednesday, the boys cooled their heels. They'd been inside of each other and on top of each other in pretty much every corner of the bar, but Ramon shrugged it off. He was just having fun, he said, but Frank—both of them still called him Frank even though they knew his real name now—felt their attraction to each other in a deeper place inside of him. It was simple and true— he came in looking for Shelley, not expecting to start anything with Ramon. She didn't know about Ramon and Frank, but of course Ramon knew about her. So, now that she was here, it seemed right for Frank and Shelley to be together. But feelings are feelings and, when they burn, you can't stop them even if you try.

She sat up in bed and went over to the purse she'd slung over the dining room chair. It wasn't one of those dainty little things but a proper big shoulder bag, the kind you can carry your whole life inside of. She took out a wad of bills that had to be a few thousand dollars, if not more, and held it out to him. He pushed the money back. His rent was due weekly in this flop house, not monthly so it was too much. She said to keep it so he has something extra and didn't have to worry. He didn't feel right about that but she insisted. The money wasn't even hers. It was barely anyone's, really. It only made sense. He wasn't quite ready to take it so she shoved it under the mattress, and they made love again, this time with all that cash underneath them.

The truth is that none of it was making any sense anymore. Living like this. Hiding out to be together. Being no one in particular. No job, no reputation to protect, no prospects. And worst of all, no ambition because, after trying hard to be on the up and up for his whole life, he'd ultimately learned that everything leads nowhere. When he talked like that she knew he was falling into that kind of hole he drops into, and that's when she decided to tell him again that she had a plan.

She was keeping their relationship a secret, and it wasn't because her husband was jealous like she told him the first time they left the bar together, when she insisted they come here to his apartment instead of the hotel. Manny didn't care about her in that way anymore but he wouldn't let her go either. She'd had affairs before and she let Manny knew all about them. He kept tabs on her but not for the reasons anyone would think.

She'd been looking for a way out; someone she could trust. He remembered her saying that the first day they met and here she was saying it again. She had been hanging out in Ramon's bar, sure she could never find the right guy, and why would she, in a place like that? But the dog had been sick for so long. The bar was across the street from the vet. She would go in there when the dog was getting treatments and she started thinking maybe this was where she would find her guy. No one would know her, no one would know anyone she met there. She needed someone she could trust but he also had to be someone no one could trace back to her. It couldn't be anyone Manny knew. It couldn't be anyone that had been seen with her, if questions started being asked.

Her eyes burned with excitement now, her pacing about and turning for emphasis causing her bobbed hair to bounce with each gesture, as she talked, faster and more deliberately.

That's why she only left the bar with him that one time and why she didn't want them to go back there. That's why she takes cabs to the corner and makes sure they leave before she walks the extra block to his flat. That's why they can't go out to dinner or the movies or even the grocery store together. That's why she never stays over and why she has to go home or to the hotel every night. Because if this is going to work, no one can know they know each other.

She looked him right in the eye now and said she knew it was him the minute he sat down on the grass and cried with her in the sculpture garden. He had a softness. That's when she knew she could finally start all over. And now she wanted him to know how he could start all over, too. But when she said there was only one person who could spoil it all because there really was only one person who could put them together, he knew exactly who that was and started worrying about exactly what she was going to ask of him next.

That's when she blindsided him with the gift he never saw coming. She said they really needed a third person and she thought they could convince Ramon to join them. That's the worm that put him firmly on the hook, a fish being pulled out of a polluted swamp and dumped into a pot of fresh water for safe transport. This was a rescue, he thought, not a trap. He was so happy inside for the first time in — he couldn't remember how long — and so he grabbed her and kissed her, and she knew he was saying yes to all of it without even knowing what they were about to do.

FIVE

Once upon a time if you were paranoid, you had secret cameras hidden all over the place so you could catch anyone trying to rip you off. Now, in the age of the internet, you want to make sure no one has any evidence that can be used against you, later, should anything go wrong. Think about it. Your house is the only private place you can control. So, no cameras anywhere. In fact, no cameras allowed. That's why, she told them both, we could get away with it. We would wear masks. And try to say as little as possible because, yes, he would be there and we'd have to beat the shit out of him, too.

That was the kicker. The "too" part, because it meant she was asking "us" to rough her up in front of him for veracity's sake. It only happened rarely that all the cash was at the house, but also, like she told him earlier, it was buried all over the back yard. The guys would drop it off at the house for a night, giving Manny time to skim some, and then the two of them would bury that together. No help, because he didn't trust anyone else.

And man oh man, burying anything is a fucking chore. Manny watches lots of old movies and he always says there's nothing funnier than a plot where they bury a body in what looks like eight feet deep by six feet long and four-plus feet wide because, she can tell you from experience, digging a little three by three hole to bury a suitcase one-foot down takes every bit of strength two not-so-young people have got.

Anyway, when that part is done, in the morning, he would make her shower again while he loaded the Escalade, so she wouldn't smell of dirt. Then she would drive the rest of it, solo, to a storage facility where she was the only one in the company outside of Manny who knew the location and had the code. That's where the mother lode of all the money is, before it gets moved again.

A month or so later when for sure no one is watching, she meets a non-FDIC armored truck that will retrieve marijuana cash from the storage unit and then they move it somewhere else, she doesn't know where. But there are cameras there at the storage place. It's a bigger haul, but you'd never get away with it. This is why Manny keeps an eye on her. Not jealousy. Not love. Not even some sick need to control someone. It's because she's important. Because she's the mule.

So here's what she wanted them to do: she always knows the day because it's the last day of every month and the only day he makes sure she's home. She'll tip them off so they can show up and "surprise" her and Manny. No need for real guns because Manny doesn't keep any at the house. Like she said, he's a movie fan, and he says you can't have a gun in the plot or someone ends up using it and usually the one who gets shot is the one who owns the piece. He's always said if you need someone shot, you hire someone to do it.

You two can have fake guns, she said, just for threatening, to make Manny and her do whatever you say until you get violent. That's when you'd tie them both up. Only do it right, because you've got all the time in the world. No one else ever comes to the house unannounced and it's out in the middle of nowhere on purpose. Then you'll notice the map, the map has to be out right before the digging starts. So now you know, you can take more money than you first thought. However much you can carry. And that's why there needs to be two of you. So you can beat them up and tie them up and so you have enough manpower to dig and load and drive away.

There were more details about the getaway and the splitting up and the house in Palm Springs but she clearly had thought this out so well, he knew she'd lay it all out again for him later anyway. His ears were ringing now, and his fingers felt numb, in that way where you can't really focus because you are having what people call an out-of-body experience. That both describes it and fails to describe it because in a way the only thing you *can* feel is your carcass, pulsating and refusing to function. The rest of it—the being here on this earth, the reality of time and the continuum of your place in history, or lack thereof—all of that goes away.

The only instance that ever happened to him before was when he won Class Singer at Le Conte Junior High, on a path to duplicate that honor at Hollywood High a few years later. When he went forward to accept the award in front of everyone, all fluid just ran out of him. He stood there, staring out at the crowd, wishing he had words and all that came out were gurgles and spittle. The whole of the student body laughed at him and thank the Goddess Fortuna they were all graduating so he didn't have to endure the ridicule the next day at school.

Singing made him popular with the girls but most of the guys hated him. He was pretty and a little fey, and shitty at sports, all of which spells "kick me" when you're thirteen. People think growing up in Hollywood is glamorous but that's Beverly Hills. The Boulevard of Dreams had long ago evolved into mean streets. Even at the middle school level, there was a black gang who abbreviated themselves in their taggings as R13 and a Latino gang who drew theirs as C14. Either group would jump you if you walked through their territory on the quad, no matter what color your skin. They each ruled one set of bathrooms off the yard too, so if you had to go, you waited and raised your hand during class to use one of the bathrooms inside the neutral zones. If it sounds like a prison, it looked like one too, with hot asphalt to stand on, and chain link fences surrounding the campus to keep the ccriminals inside for the seven hours a day they were to be held captive. For survival, the white trash kids and their smattering of non-gang related ethnic friends stood behind the toughest boy and girl in school, John and Winter.

The gangs dubbed them, with uncharacteristic irony, The Surfers because, even though they tended to ditch school *en masse* and jump the #4 RTD bus down Santa Monica to the beach, not a one of them actually knew how to catch a wave. Their crimes ranged from public transit hopping to petty shoplifting to sneaking in the back door of the Chinese Theater to get high watching R-rated movies. A few of them became particularly adept at fishing change from news kiosks by attaching chewing gum to the end of a straw and wiggling the quarters upwards. A couple were more bold and took to stealing Olde English 800 six packs from the liquor store while their co-conspirators distracted the counter help with large purchases of Now & Later candies.

To commemorate the moniker, one badass kid with balls took a shoplifted sharpie to the walls of a co-ed toilet on the first floor of the main building and scribbled out all of The Surfers names. Boys down one wall. Girls down the other.

Below the exhaustive list of all the girls who were part of the unofficial mob of young hoodlum wannabes—Winter, Suzanne, Carmen, Lisa, Jennifer, Lana, Averil, Jen, Gina, Janeen, Chaimi, Stephanie, Fauna, Donna, Liz, Elizabeth, Robin, Katie, Ada, Pam and on—at the bottom, was his name, the real one he hated, Babe, but in all caps, which he saw as a kind of rejection and exaltation via the same gesture. He felt both embarrassed and notorious, an outsider on the inside, which might well describe him to this day.

"The Surfers" sounds innocuous enough, unless you saw Winter beat that one rival girl to a bloody pulp to prove that everyone should leave her friends alone. For some reason he never fully understood, Winter decided the little kid who could sing was her best friend, so Babe was officially hands off, unless you wanted to suffer her wrath. She drop-kicked one boy who she overheard offering up advice that if he didn't have sex with a girl by the time he was thirteen, Babe was gonna grow up to be a fag.

The closest he got to having to be in a fight on this daily battleground was the time some senior kid named Claudio screwed up a verse in dress rehearsal during his solo on Three Dog Night's "The Show Must Go On," the closing anthem of this year's circus-themed Young World Follies. The drama teacher, Mr. Crumb, had been so impressed by the underclassman's audition for the troupe (Frank sang the Gary Wright song "Dream Weaver" to a standing ovation), that Crumb split Claudio's solo and gave half of it to the new kid as a kind of negative encouragement/punishment. Claudio's henchmen Ian McSomethingorother and Roy O'thisorthat sent out the word that they would Nair that little fucker's hair if they caught him alone. Winter shut it down. And she commemorated the moment two years later in his senior yearbook, writing, "Never forget 'Dream Weaver,' the song that started it all."

Right now, all he could hear was "This Guy's in Love with You" playing on the jukebox. The Herb Alpert version, where his voice cracks at the end when he warbles that he might just die if his love is unrequited. He found himself staring right at Ramon as he involuntarily sang along, softly, as if to himself, to think, but maybe it was to keep him from thinking.

That's when Ramon reached behind the bar and pulled out a handgun, to show he was in. Shelley stared at it for what felt like a minute, afraid to look anywhere else for fear of changing the direction of the moment. The hair on the back of Frank's neck stood up and his ball sack tightened. He was a music teacher. A singer. Okay a lousy one, or maybe not lousy, just not good enough, but that's how he identified himself if someone asked. He was a bit of a Lothario, he would tell you at a party, a slut even, and he drank too much, sure. He was up to here with feeling like the bottom of someone's shoe, which is why he quit his job, signing his resignation note, "Damn the torpedoes, full speed ahead," like a man who knew that calmer heads would see he was advancing towards certain destruction. At this point, his girlfriend, if you could call her that, was paying his rent, so the likelihood of coming out on top in life was small at best. So the question hung there, smoke in the air. Could he do this? He blinked, sighed and a tear rolled down Shelley's cheek.

There's only one part she can't figure out: how she and Manny get free. How they don't just end up laying there, eventually starving to death if they are properly tied up. What Ramon suggested next was so twisted and rank, she knew it would work. She looked at Frank and nodded in that way that says she is willing. Her blank black eyes were pleading with him to say he was too. She even whispered the obligatory "C'mon, Babe," calling him by his real name—unless she was using it like it gets used most of the time. At this point, he wished his name was Frank and that he wasn't really himself because it frightened him to know that not only could Babe do this, he could make it sell.

SIX

Everything went exactly as she said, until it didn't. And that started from before it started. It was the first time Ramon had seen Babe's lonely apartment, and so he looked around. Empty bottles, take-out food containers, dirty clothes in one corner. The only real sign of personality were his LPs and his all-in-one turntable that kept the silence at bay, tuned to the oldies station 24-7 unless he put on a record. Ramon threw the remains of yesterday's Subway lunch in the trash, clearing way to put a plastic bag full of clothes on the table. From Target. That's what Shelley said to do: go to Target and buy generic black trousers, t-shirts, underwear, shoes, and socks with cash. 100% untraceable.

But to get into said outfits, they had to strip down. And when the guys took off their own clothes, there was no avoiding the problem. There's nothing you can do when you are drawn to someone in that way. The room gets smaller. The air swells and thins. Skin warms.

Ramon started it by moving close. He knew what he was doing when he folded his pants and carried them over towards the table. Babe didn't have to turn around to know Ramon was looking at his back and his shoulders. When you want someone to touch you,

you can feel their eyes on you, even with your face turned away. When Babe stopped moving around the room, well, it became obvious he wasn't "getting dressed." He was standing there, frozen, knowing Ramon was behind him, willing him to lift the back of his hand forward and run it down his neck.

The smell of a person you desire overwhelms all logic. You know you shouldn't turn and face him. You know you shouldn't sigh like that, making that noise as you breathe in through your nose and then exhale slowly through your mouth, telling him without saying anything, that yes, you do want him to take the step that would put him right up against you. And your fingers shouldn't roam over his rib cage. Your thumb shouldn't slip down his oblique to trace his pelvis bone or hook under the band of his boxers. There's no way you'll push him away if he lifts your chin and kisses you now. You've been together before so there's hardly a look that has to be exchanged before the two of you swim beyond the point of turning back from this. You're on the floor, hands everywhere. Mouths open and giving. You're sucking in his air only it feels like water because you're aware you could be drowning. There's spit and there's thrusting. Rolling and wrestling. Positions you've tried before and some you've seen in pictures, or movies you feel guilty about watching. You find yourself acting overwhelmed to make the other one reach out to rescue you, and with your gaze you tell him you're not afraid to stay under, and you're the one who takes him down with you, deeper. Overwhelmed. Everything disappears but him. You disappear too. You're lost. Gone. Obliterated. All the things you know you should be doing to prevent this from happening and all the things you know you shouldn't be allowing become powerless against the tide, the undertow, carrying you out to sea. That's when you slip under the surface for good, where you decide: it's time to relax and stop fighting. You admit you are weak, sense that there is something stronger than you. If this current refuses to release you, then you're willing to accept that. You think maybe you can grab some of your own air and so you try. And then it happens. He reaches in and grabs you by the heart and you both gasp and push back away from each other while you simultaneously grab hold, and in the span of a few extended and excruciating seconds, your blood rushes hot until your lungs cease to be shocked by the trauma. You float. Your chest settles. You find yourself looking at...nothing. At the white ceiling, at the texture of the paint. The cracks. Cracks you never saw before. He asks if you're okay and you look away from him and wonder what the hell he means by that. Do you need to be? What if you aren't okay, you wonder. Or worse, what if you're not and he is.

They dressed in silence. He was feeling on the verge of tears (which could not happen, no matter what) when Ramon reached over, turned him around again, kissed him and held his face. That's the moment he washed back up onto the shore, exhausted, exhilarated, and suddenly more ready to do this job than he was in those lonesome hours before Ramon walked in tonight. Not because he was considering that he might be falling in love. Though, admittedly, to even have the thought that you are or are not in that terrible state means that miserable little cherub has likely fired darts at you.

Babe was near certain he was not idiotic enough to draw lines connecting what just happened between them to any sort of potential or lasting nonsense. What he felt, for the first time in a long time, he told himself, was not love. It was only that things might not be meaningless after all.

His ears stopped ringing. A song was playing and he realized the stereo must have been on this whole time. Music is something you should turn off during monumental events in your life because hit lyrics never cease to land in ways that are overripe with cliché. If the record went gold or, God forbid, platinum, you can bet your life is about to be reduced to thoughts and feelings a million teenage girls felt the first time they heard the tune. Ramon put his arms around his waist and swayed. Dancing? They were going to dance? He sang along, softly, into Ramon's ear though he didn't know he was doing it.

Habit. ("*Chances are...*")

Because the occasion was certainly now feeling way too cheesy, he spun Ramon out into a twirl and looked him in the eye as he sang the next part, sporting an ear to ear goofy grin, and with every intention of making sure Ramon would think it impossible he meant any of the words. He even took care to mock Johnny Mathis' soft and lilting cadence, sounding even slightly feminine to cover up all of the manly crimes they just committed.

Ramon hit him in the shoulder, as if to say he didn't want to be made fun of, so Babe smiled with a bit more generosity. He told Ramon they didn't want to be late. They gathered up the rest of their things but when Ramon took the gun out of his bag and set it on the table, out in the open, the gravity of the evening set out before them, split wide like an ill-bandaged wound.

SEVEN

In theory, it was a simple plan. Tonight, she said, the money would be there. They'd creep into the house without any noise. They'd steal into position fast, take Manny down first with the butt of a gun but the girl would come at them like a banshee so she'd get no mercy. That would get Manny deliberating about who in his organization might be able to put this much together. First, he'd run through potential disgruntled workers, maybe thinking two of them followed him home. Thoughts would wander closer to home, to Shelley.

That's why they'd have to let her have it, hard. They all three agreed Ramon had to do that, especially since Babe had to perform the last part, the horrible act to sell the whole thing. With Ramon's accent, he wasn't allowed to utter a word. It made him more frightening, some kind of silent monster. Babe could speak but leaning towards the monosyllabic. As few words as possible. Quick, clean, mean. And as long as they stuck to her plan, in less than a week's time, Shelley would meet them at their designated hide outs: Babe sequestered quietly in her Palm Springs house, and Ramon tucked safely and anonymously away with the money, 30 minutes to the north in Desert Hot Springs.

Assuming they would do exactly what she said, everything would go exactly according to the plan.

That was the theory.

Sure enough, as soon as he was bound and gagged, Manny started studying everything about them. Their gaits. Their bearings. Thickness of legs. Distance from torso to waist. No skin was showing. Even under the masks, they wore cheap sunglasses. Walmart, he thought. Or Venice boardwalk. Maybe a liquor store on the way here. Maybe the one at the bottom of the hill. They didn't seem drunk so they weren't sloppy, which means they probably thought far enough into the future not to leave a detail like that to last minute chance, but there was no reason not to go into the liquor store to ask. Add all that up, and they were smart. Educated, he guessed. Maybe the silent one is foreign. Anyway, that's why they threw on more lights when they came in. So they could see with those shades over their eyes. Again, he thought, smart.

It was well choreographed. That brought him back to Shelley. But her eyes went wide at him and he wondered what the fuck she was trying to say. Through the blood dripping down his brow he could see her flicking a panicked look towards where the map was spread out, right in front of the two thieves. Now he wanted her to fucking stop it before one of them spotted her antics. He gave a calm nod so she'd know he got the message.

That's when the taller one stopped in his tracks and hit the shoulder of the other one. Their backs were to Manny and Shelley, shoving money into an army duffel, so there was no way they saw her, Manny hoped. He unwittingly stomped his feet and screamed through the duct tape covering his mouth. If ever there was a sign they were on to something, he just telegraphed it. Manny wasn't aware, but of course they already knew what they were looking for.

Babe studied the map and his heart raced. This was it, he thought. Whatever they were shoving in the bag was a lot but think of that times—what, a hundred, a thousand—if every X meant they buried the same amount of loot. Loot! He laughed at himself out loud for thinking of such a colloquialism and then stifled it. It was too much. Shelley had already told them they'd never be able to marshal it all and they'd never be able to come back. It was cash and carry time. More tape, more mono-syllabic threats of violence. More posturing, and then they both left the room with the map.

What Ramon had done to her hurt like hell so it wasn't hard for Shelley to cry. She figured Manny wasn't feeling a thing, his adrenaline running high, but from her vantage point, she could see he was bleeding from the temple. Shelley knew that they couldn't be left there in the room or they'd likely die. They lay there for what felt like hours before she eventually fell asleep.

She awoke suddenly when the tape ripped off her face and was relieved to see them because it meant they were going to go through with everything, as planned. Of course, if this whole scenario were real, this would be when the dread would have set into her because the thieves should not have come back inside the house.

Manny, not in on the set-up like her, did shake with the terror. The only reason for them to come inside, after digging up that kind of money, would be that, out there in the woods, their greed overwhelmed any remaining sense of right and wrong.

These men came back to kill them, he decided. And he was going to be second, not first, which was noxious. But why would they un-tie her? This made no sense. Until it did. Until the fucking bastard dragged her out of the room by her hair and threw her down in the hallway and got on top of her. All he could see of them were feet. The other guy was watching him, with the gun on him, as if it mattered because not only was he bound so that he couldn't move, he was indeed being murdered, watching it. Or what he could see of it. Tiny, broken, pretty Shelley underneath that motherfucker in black. His lust, out of control. Her feet. Her shoes. The only thing left of her, the tanned leather bottom of her penny loafers, her soles scuffed from normal daily wear.

Whoever these guys were, they were taking everything from him. In that instant, Manny knew it was all his fault. For making her be the mule. For thinking this would somehow finish any other way but this. How else could it end? Who the fuck cares now how these two cocksuckers figured it all out. Who cares. Who cares. That's all that kept running through his mind as he tried not to look. Who cares.

In the hallway and safely out of range from Manny, Babe lifted his ski mask and sunglasses so she could see that it was really him. Acting awful is one thing, but she appreciated seeing his pretty amber eyes. It normalized the whole crazy endeavor they had gotten themselves into. Her eyes said everything to him because both of them knew she couldn't touch him or tip Manny off in any way whatsoever.

After being with Ramon so soon before, he feared that when this moment came he wouldn't be able to do much, but the night and the money were powerful aphrodisiacs. He played his part dreadfully well, gripping her skirt up in a ball around her waist and, if you happened upon it, you'd think it was the ugliest thing that could ever happen to a woman.

Manny saw the taller thief get up and leave first. Then the other one, the silent conspirator did something remarkable. He pulled Shelley's skirt down over her knees before he followed, down the stairs, and out the front door with a bang.

The distant sound of the car starting up was conversely unremarkable. A rental, probably. Or stolen. That could lead to a clue. Tracks in the dirt might pinpoint a make or model. And boot prints. There could be some on the stairs or outside.

With all of this running in his head, he made the mistake of looking again at Shelley's feet, askew, one loafer on, one off, a toe sticking out of a ripped stocking, still, motionless. With it all over, in the silence of the empty, violated household, he could hear her frail, tired weeping, and that's when the dysphoria took him over. Tracks. Cars. Who did it. Who fucking cares?

The truth is that Shelley bore no tears but he couldn't see that. She surprised even herself with the performance. Fabricated or not, it was an exhausting night and it was hours before she crawled over and freed one of Manny's hands. By this time, though, he had passed out. She knew that was dangerous, with such a blow to the head and, of course, she couldn't call the police or an ambulance, so she called one of Manny's guys. She knew that when he came to, he'd be furious that she'd invited someone else to the house, but that was going to help her convince him it was over. She couldn't live like this. Not even Manny could expect her to. Or maybe it wasn't over. Maybe she just needed time. Alone. There was the Palm Springs house he bought her. She wanted to drive there. By herself. The idea was that if she wasn't running, he wouldn't chase her. Anyway, that's what she was going to say when he finally reemerged from his sleep. But Manny had slipped into a coma so she ended up not having to say anything at all.

EIGHT

The key was where she said it would be, under the fake rock by the ocotillo in the front yard. Being a criminal now meant he could evaluate things for himself, like what a bad hiding spot that is. First of all, a neighbor might see you retrieve it, and now they would know how to get in. Second of all, a fake rock looks like a fake rock. What else is gonna be in it but the key to the house.

The Kings Point community has forty-four International Style family residences where each one looks essentially the same as the next one. Clean lines. No ornamentation. All straight angles and glass. They blend one into the other so beautifully that sometimes residents come home tipsy and pull close to the wrong house before they realize their remote opened their garage next door. Add it all up and it equals anonymity. Plus, where this Palm Springs enclave rests, at the absolute bottom of town, sandwiched between two golf courses, one that no one uses, makes it isolated in plain sight.

The lights in the house are all on timers so it won't look suspect, she told him, when there are suddenly signs of life. Go in, be quiet about it, and if some Gladys Kravitz gets nosey before she gets there, you're a cousin of the owners. The HOA doesn't allow short term rentals, but family is allowed anytime.

The first thing he wanted was a shower. He was covered in sex and dirt and the sweat of hard work. The quiet of an empty house is so startling, though. You feel watched by ghosts lurking in the silence, especially when you've done wrong. So he didn't feel comfortable adding further vulnerability by stripping down naked, not just yet.

He wandered through the place and it was one of those decorating jobs you know was paid for. Cookie cutter "Design Out of Reach" modernism, as he called it. It was clear that no one went to a vintage store and said, "I love this chair," or decided to support some artist from a local gallery. No, this was overpriced simplicity. Eames, Noguchi, Baughman. There was even one of those ubiquitous huge framed "Poolside Gossip" photos by Slim Aarons, but from the outtakes, not the classic one, so it reeked of trying to feel fresh. Why not just hang up Marilyn from the last shoot where she's nude behind the orange and yellow scarf, and a wall-sized "Palm Springs Weekend" poster and be done with it, he thought.

He still felt filthy, so he went to the bathroom and washed his face. The mistake there was that you look up and you're staring at yourself. Besides slivers and glimpses he tried to avoid in the rear view mirror, he hadn't yet had to confront the day. So, how do you feel, "Frank," he asked himself and the answer surprised him. He was ok. More than ok. He felt good. And so he took that shower after all.

Showers have great acoustics, so it's no myth that you sound better. You can push to sing notes that are hard to hit elsewhere and they come together in the way your voice bounces off the walls and resonates back inside your head. Wasn't it the Flintstones where Fred discovered Barney could sing like an angel alone in his bathroom? They took him on the road only he couldn't perform in normal life, so they had to cart a bathtub around on tour. Something like that. Then it all went awry, the way things always do on television. That's entertainment. The plan gets all screwed up so the characters can learn an important lesson. Life is not like that, he thought, as he sang out, with perfect pitch and timbre, no song in particular, just a long clear-ended do-re-mi-fa-so-la-ti-dough....

The plan was that Ramon would hold all the money so if someone got caught, it'd be him. It was Shelley's suggestion but Ramon agreed to it because, in the end, he had the least to lose. He had not a dime to his name. Suddenly "undocumented" had such a positive ring to it: no paperwork, no history to track.

They were supposed to hang out in L.A. a day or so, long enough so as not to arouse suspicion in case anyone had put two and two together and was watching them. Then, Ramon would tell his bar boss—who, shock of all shocks, hired him without papers because he had a terrible crush on him—that he was going home to Mexico. His "American experiment" was a failed one. There was nothing here for him. It would be easy to say, because it wasn't a lie — except for the maybe millions of dollars in the trunk of his car, and the gringo singer he had to know was in love with him.

The big question right now was would Ramon roll up into Desert Hot Springs with all that cash, with no one to stop him, or would he run? Because the sinking feeling haunting Babe as the water poured over him was not one of a robber afraid to get caught or double-crossed, but of a fool who had shown his heart too soon. If Ramon asked that same question he had asked himself in the mirror, Babe wondered, what would be his answer? How did Ramon feel?

It seemed kosher to swim some laps in the pool. A neighbor might notice but he had his story ready. And being submerged was an immediate relief. No sound. Nothing to look at but that blue-white void. His mind, though, wouldn't obey his demands to go blank. It raced and repeated, paralleling the strokes and the breathing, up and out of the water, down and around the same details, all the things that should go right, but could, at any juncture, go terribly wrong.

Shelley was not expected right away. She had to make things look good before she could ask for her time alone. She had to act troubled from the incident. Hurt. Confused. Violated, not just by that vicious and awful man, but by the whole situation. By not being able to talk about it. By living with someone who she was pretty sure didn't even really like her anymore. The whole plan was hers, so she wouldn't betray it, he was near certain.

That meant that if Ramon could escape his amorous boss without triggering any trouble, they could have time like those first reckless few weeks together in the empty bar, before Shelley came back into the picture. But now all the "if's" swirled around him. If Ramon showed up. If he felt the same way. If no one got caught. If she finally came and was reasonable. If she would let them go. Why wouldn't she? He'd done everything she wanted. They got out with the money. She was free. And isn't that all anyone wants in life, to have money and be free? Even he had to laugh at that.

And then the song came back in his head so he sung it out loud to himself, underwater, his breath bubbling up to the surface:

Ninety-nine miles from L.A.

We're laughing, we're loving,

Please be there.

NINE

Desert Hot Springs is an ugly town, and worse it's a sham. Advertised as one of the rare places in the world with naturally occurring hot and cold mineral springs, people come thinking it will be a resort, with pools of healing water where hope flows eternal. In reality, it's a smattering of exhausted motels and hotels with over-chlorinated man-made hot tubs. A few do have bona fide taps into the natural waters below ground, but their decades-old patched and re-painted cement ponds fail to live up to any promise of spiritual rejuvenation. Wide indecorous streets feel dead under the relentless heat. Where Palm Springs charms, Desert Hot Springs thuds. No views. No shops. No shade.

In the 1940s, this was the town where buses dropped newly released ex-cons and it has never risen out from under that legacy. But it's less murderous than it is petty. With just under half of the population struggling below the poverty level, the people who live here perch daily on a verge of doing something untoward just to get by—like stealing some lady's phone out of her hand, or breaking the window of your SUV to pinch your change.

Tweakers hang out on the fringes of gas stations foisting their dirty-water window washing services upon unsuspecting travelers so they can filch whatever they can grab out of your billfold when you're dumb enough to open it to give a tip. When they tire of that low-stakes charade, they cluster in sun-drenched asphalt lots, sharing an ill-begotten 40-ouncer or a family-size bottle of Thunderbird. High desert weather is cruel in both directions—either far too hot for humans, or way too windy cold to be shirtless wearing cut-offs and flip-flops outside the KFC, unless you happen to be high on a speed, crack and coffee combo.

A normal person wouldn't feel safe parking at the Rite-Aid, much less braving entry into any number of liquor stores masquerading as convenience marts. And if a stray bachelorette on a spa getaway does find herself inside the corner Lucky Shoppe, you can bet she'll have to wait to purchase her Evian until the regular patrons are finished redeeming yesterday's $5 California Lotto win in trade for today's losing Scratch-n-Play game tickets.

For reasons unrelated to that bottom feeding gen-pop, Babe knew it was risky to be driving through Desert Hot Springs so soon after the heist, but what if, by chance, he could run into Ramon, accidentally on purpose? What harm could there be in that, he asked himself. Of course, the answer was plain. The plan. The plan. The plan. Shelley's dictate remained resolute because they all agreed: no one was to get in touch with any of the others until the three of them could convene. Finding Ramon before the arranged group rendezvous risked bringing some hapless witness' eyes in their direction that later could testify, "Yes, I saw them together. The Mexican and the professor. They sat very close, whispering. You might even say intimate. So, yes, your honor, there is no doubt in my mind they knew each other from before."

Cruising the streets was useless. It might feel like a one horse village, with the main drag, Dillon Avenue, running like an artery opened by a stent to the heart of the town—a false artery that leads past un-welcoming honkey-tonks advertising Ladies Night Every Night and Karaoke Wednesdays—but Desert Hot Springs is home to more than 40,000 people. In August, night temperatures hold firm at 100 degrees. There's no way you're going to see any kind of friendly or familiar face walking down the empty sidewalks in the middle of week. People leave their air-conditioned apartments and drive their air-conditioned cars to air-conditioned drinking establishments. It made sense to stop because, he could tell himself, he wanted a cold beverage and maybe he could even sing a song.

Locals tend to either hate tourists or love them for brightening up what would otherwise be another boring night of the same old same old, and Babe felt fortunate this pot-bellied red-faced saloon owner belonged to the former group. He didn't want to be chatted up by some half-wit posing some basic query but really wanting to spew his own useless life story, and he most certainly didn't want to answer questions like, What Brings a Guy Like You to Our Little Edge of the World?

Rudeness can be a most welcome behavioral trait in a bartender when you just want to be left to your own agenda. The guy conducted himself, in fact, so brusquely and impersonally—quick-pouring a to-the-rim bar tequila on the rocks without so much as looking up—that he likely couldn't have picked Babe out of a line-up an hour from now, much less in the weeks that followed should everything spiral out of control from here.

This was without a doubt the place Ramon told him about. Antlers over the bar. Wagon wheels on the walls. Barrels made into stools. Sawdust on the floor. The difficulty of communicating those words still made Babe chuckle. Ramon had to act each one of them out. "Antlers" was of course the easy one, and even now he could picture him, nude after sex, with fingers on his head, making animal sounds which Babe ridiculed him over because, really, what sound does a buck make? The detail of a foreign language escapes most of us when we study it. We might learn the word for arm and hand and finger, but what about elbow or wrist or thumb? And when you are self-taught from television, music and random flirtatious strangers, you most certainly don't learn words to describe the hackneyed decorations that might find themselves littered around a Way Out West themed watering hole.

The short time, now more than a decade ago, that Ramon spent in Desert Hot Springs was rough. He landed here right after leaving Mexico, driven in the back of a Walmart delivery truck on its way to Los Angeles from Playas de Tijuana where he grew up and went to school. Or so he thought he was going to Los Angeles. It cost him his full savings (minus two hundred dollars which he tucked into his sock) to pay for that ride but the coyote driver didn't tell him he wouldn't be able to take him the whole way. You can't just slide open your metal door in a mall in Culver City and have seven wetback *coños* crawl out, he'd said.

So when Ramon bounced from the back of the truck, expecting palm trees and beach air, he instead found the cement and foresakenness of Desert Hot Springs.

On arrival, Ramon knew some things: like that his money wouldn't last and that the good thing about a place this hot is that there's no problem sleeping outside. There were other things he didn't know: like, he didn't know much English, and he had no idea exactly how far away L.A. was from the desert. Some things he did learn quickly: like, there's no way you could walk from this armpit to the big city, and no matter how good-looking, a Latino who can't speak the local language fluently can only get work if he's willing to do manual or menial labor.

During the day, he washed dishes or dug ditches at construction sites, while at night he used what God gave him to survive, because though Desert Hot Springs has nothing even remotely like a gay bar, it does have closeted military men afraid to be seen lurking about the more open establishments of Palm Springs.

Often drunk enough to spend their grunt cash on what they really want to be doing in the gloamings off the base, those were the nights he got to sleep in a paid-up-front motel room, usually alone, believe it or not, after the Marine-in-question stole away and left him in the double bed—sprawled, spent, and flush. Those were the mornings he got a shower and a shave, and enjoyed the luxury of sitting in front of a TV, repeating aloud the dialogue from *Law & Order: SVU* re-runs on TNT. Chris Meloni was so handsome, he followed his lips with the most focus, thinking about communicating with that kind of *guapo* gringo boyfriend to pay all his bills.

When you're good at what you do, word spreads,

and before long, all Ramon had to do was hang out in the corner over by the jukebox. Eyes would meet. Message received. Alley. Money first. Maybe a grope, a sample of the goods being sold. Then, to the motel in the guy's car. More groping. Inside. Clothes, ripped off, usually fast and clumsy. Marines are in shape so it was never gross, though now and again, you'd get a self-loather and then it might get angry and distasteful for a moody spell while the trick wrestled with that. But they always wanted it. All of it. It wasn't their first time either because they knew positions they wanted to try and, every now and then, something scatological he didn't like. Violence was off limits, but it did happen a couple of times when he couldn't control those moments.

One thing about this particular form of hustle is that, though they might be dog-faced now and then, military guys are muscled, which could be a worry because, as strong as Ramon might be, they were trained fighters and could be harboring hidden traumas they only shared through this kind of reluctant vulnerability. It made the sex edgy and sometimes unfriendly, and yes, sometimes wild and unpredictably satisfying for him, so much so that it almost felt wrong to take the money.

He had regular customers, one of whom convinced himself he had fallen for Ramon. When he got shipped out, he left car keys and a signed pink slip as a tip on his last day. He wrote a note too, asking that he never tell anyone about their "affair," and pleading that Ramon never forget him because, now that he knew his mission, he was pretty sure he wouldn't be coming home alive. The next morning, Ramon drove himself to L.A.

And now? Now he was on the 10 freeway, driving that same Toyota, with a trunk full of trouble, back from whence he came.

Babe sat in Ramon's dark spot next to the jukebox, shaking uncontrollably with nervousness, watching a couple of drunk buddies mangle "Don't You Want Me, Baby?" with one of them camping it up in the girl's part. It convinced him there was no way he would get up to sing a song. Singing in public—with his voice, in a dive like this—would kill his anonymity.

He finished his drink, went out the back door into the alley, savored an imaginary drunken grope session out there, and drove to an unlit street just north of the flophouse motel Ramon described. He parked around the corner so he arrived on foot, and paid for a room for a week with Shelley's dirty cash. He sat on the bed, turned on the TV, and watched an episode of *Law & Order: SVU* on TNT.

TEN

Shelley had prepared herself for a lot of different scenarios but this was not one of them. Yet here she sat, holding Manny's hand, bedside, and playing the role of a woman who wanted him to recover. His doctor warned her: he likely would not come out of this and at some juncture, as his wife, his next of kin, she might be charged with having to make the decision to "pull the plug," as they say.

She told the doctor the story of her dog and asked if it might be more humane to just do that, now, and not let Manny suffer, but the doctor "comforted" her by explaining that in the state he's in, he feels no pain, and anyway she did not need to decide that for 48 days, at which point there would be the near-certainty of brain damage. Had he only been called sooner, she lamented, right after the head wound, maybe there would have been more chance of survival. But to have fallen into the coma, to have bled so badly, well, Shelley only wished she had not herself been so traumatized that she might have recognized sooner he needed help.

So, in that way, she knew she was safe. There would be no miracle cure. Her problem now was that she had no way to communicate with the boys and she would never get out of there on schedule with Manny in this state, still alive. If he were cognizant she had her rehearsed speech, her whole act worked up. But how callous she would look to leave his side now. Red flags flying. Every fiber in her body screamed at her to run, but her intelligence kept her in her place.

The second the doctor left Manny's bedroom, she dropped his hand to pace and think. Asphyxiation would be discovered. Poison, no way. Any kind of weaponry, obviously out of the question. Another bang to the head, in the same spot? Would that leave a new mark, and anyway, would it even do anything? Whenever she left the room one of his goons came in, so she couldn't say he must have woken during an absence of supervision, ambled into the bathroom, and drowned in the tub. Her only recourse, it seemed, was to wait. Wait until the company doctor suggested lethal injection. Her best current idea, then, was to find a way to move that date up, to get the doctor to suggest an injection of euthanization, sooner rather than later.

Did you know that in the hospital, they can't do that, and that some flat-lined patients removed from life support breathe on their own for up to two days before they finally choke to death for lack of air? The thought of Manny suffering that fresh hell sent a buzz right through her. There was, too, the possibility that while she was trying to figure out the best way to bring about his demise, Manny might just expire on his own. In any case, the core of her challenge remained the same: wait.

The one card she held was that if any one of the three of the partners broke from their bond, the others could, and likely would, turn them all in, assuming they'd bring everyone down. The joker up her sleeve, though, was that whether or not Manny died now, she could come forward as the wife who was wronged, even claim spousal imprisonment if she had to, and identify her husband's assailants, especially the one who debased her right in front of him.

She knows she's not in the will. Manny always feared being killed which meant he wrote a last testament that left everything to some stupid children's hospital—so she'd end up with a whole lot of nothing, but that's all she had before anyway. Who would believe Ramon and "Frank" (she still preferred that name to his childlike given name) that she was in on it? Two thieves, one a foreigner with a thick accent, the other a rapist. This remained her ultimate potential double cross. If they turn on her, she turns on them, hard.

For fuck's sake, she thought as she weighed her options, what a bad plan. The only good plan is for the whole thing to go off.

Out the window, to the backyard, she could see that

Manny's guys were clearing the place of all the extra cash. The heist had left the backyard looking like a minefield, so Manny was pretty much busted now by his colleagues for all the years of skimming. They were getting back money they didn't know they were missing. Of course they'd get greedy and think that whatever the thieves made off with should be theirs as well. Everyone told Shelley, in so many words and actions, that she wasn't a suspect. But minds wander, so she truly had to behave the way your average person would think a grieving wife would behave.

How did I get here, she wondered aloud. The voicing of it brought a knock from a concerned goon in the hall, so she had to tell him she was sorry, she was talking to herself. He wrinkled his brow in empathy and went back to his post. Everyone looked at her now like damaged goods, which in her estimation was hilarious, because the sex with Frank in the hallway might have been some of the best she ever had. So taboo. So wrong. And so public with both Manny and hopefully Ramon watching. She had to act like she didn't want it, like it was her downfall as a woman, but what was new about that? She had been doing that her whole life.

Men are so stupid. They think women don't enjoy the act, can't throw themselves into a twisted moment, can't want. If a woman does convince some lover of her complexity, her archetype gets reversed on her, from Madonna to Whore, like she can't hold multiple beings within. You know why men think like that? Because they can't do it themselves. Men are simple and unidimensional and they have zero imagination for any possibilities outside of their own experience. That's also why women baffle men. How confusing can it be, to understand someone isn't like you?

Even Frank, who seemed better than the rest, said to her about men and women, trying to relate: It's like the blind leading the blind. You aren't blind, she told him. You have your eyes closed. He came back with a quick retort: Fine, then, you're the blind one, he said. Then, being smart, added: Even if my eyes are closed, I have insight. It was a clever professorial turn of phrase, she gave him that. But then, as she considered her retort, he rolled over and went to sleep, without waiting for her, like a man does after being fully satisfied, not worrying about his partner's fulfillment, assuming his own gratification was somehow hers as well.

Out of the blue, Manny gurgled and swallowed and began to cough uncontrollably. Again, the noise brought the goons into the room and because it looked bad, they woke the doctor up in his room downstairs as well. For a moment she thought he was coming out of the coma but when they calmed him, or perhaps he simply calmed himself and returned to his odd vegetative state, the doctor told her what happened. The path for air to enter our lungs, he said, is very close to the esophageal sphincter, the correct entry point for food and liquids. Your brain usually makes you do the right things, sending air to the lungs and food, drink and yes, even saliva to the esophagus. Unconsciously. So we never really think about it unless we swallow wrong and cough.

Conversely, millions of people with brain diseases, including those with Alzheimer's, Parkinson's, Lou Gehrig's disease, stroke, multiple sclerosis and, like Manny here, traumatic head injury, suffer impaired swallowing that neither the cerebrum nor the medulla oblongata can control. In layman's terms, Manny is unable to protect his lungs in the way that a healthy person can. So it's good this happened. Now she knows: he is at serious risk.

Crisis averted, they left her alone again with her tormentor. She looked at Manny and patted his hand, thanking him for giving her the solution. He could drown in his own spit. Burn out his lungs. Catch pneumonia and die. And she would be released.

ELEVEN

Ramon started the drive thinking he'd do everything that was asked but when he saw the casino at Cabazon, something cold came over him. Maybe the flashing lights telling him he could Be A Winner Tonight increased the temptation. Whatever the reason, he drove all the way to Calexico before he decided not to do it. All he had to do was slip over the border into Mexicali, and he knew it would all be his. Then, as long as he went deep into the country and avoided the big cities, how would they ever find him? Americans don't know the first thing about Mexico beyond the vacation spots. So why did he pull over to the side of the road, having second thoughts?

His hateful bastard of a father had zero regard for right or wrong, so there's no way he got any conscience from him, and his vagabond mother was twice the operator he was. Together, the two of them ran scams on over-confident tourists. They stole every peso they earned. Ramon swore as a young man not to be like them, but to look in the mirror was to see his parents. His mother, Jilda, was cursed with looks that people kindly called striking, while on her son, that same strong face would forever make his life easier. While luck meant he did not get his father Ramon Senior's unhappy countenance, he did get his broad shoulders and strapping frame.

From a young age, he saw the attraction a certain kind of man had towards him. During the years that everyone called him Junior, any attention remained innocent. Ok, not always so innocent, but no one reached over any lines without his permission, even if Ramon gave them the encouragement they wanted from such a pretty boy.

When he turned fifteen, he grew six inches and no one called the towering abundant man "Junior" anymore. Not when they kissed him, not when they were in love with him, and certainly not when they cried over losing him. Somehow the adventurous part of Jilda came through in that way and he adhered to it: he simply and intuitively despised being boxed in. If he had been at all open to being owned, even temporarily, he might have had his choice of any number of lovers that could have given him a better life.

The local college, CIDH Universidad, offered four majors and Ramon chose hotel management, thinking it might offer him a way out of Mexico. What he really learned in school was that people want to give things to people who are beautiful. They also, however, want something in return, and that something, to Ramon, felt like a chunk of his soul. *Follado por un pez*, as they say. Fucked by a fish. That lesson got absorbed in college, not from a lowly teacher but from the Dean himself. He put Ramon up in a Tijuana flat near his own house because he thought this way he could keep his impressive thing all for himself, caged, showering him in money for clothes and cars, and the promise of his continuing education.

Of course he had his own key to Ramon's apartment, and of course he found Ramon there one night with not one, but three other guys, sleeping, limbs intertwined in and around each other like only happened after an all-night wrestling match where you weren't quite sure at any given time who was inside who. The Dean threw him out, crying as he did it, crushed to his core that Ramon didn't want to hold back that part of himself just for him.

It might seem like bartering flesh for money teaches you dishonesty when in reality you learn a certain system of ethics. Hustling isn't dishonest, Ramon told himself for all those years after being expelled from his studies, because it contains a fair exchange. He got by, up into his thirties, by refusing to give away what he could trade on. And now, in his forties, he figured it could only last so much longer. Sure, men still wanted to possess him, that likely would never change, but what was different now was that he himself ran across guys who he wanted to be with, without wanting anything in return, and usually those were the ones where he was on more common footing financially.

Like Babe, for instance. Why not? The guy barely paid his own way on a teacher's salary so he clearly had no design or ability to start wanting to control anyone. Ramon liked his looks and his body, and they shared an equal feeling of being inexorably drawn together the minute they were alone. Plus, he liked the way Babe sang softly in his ear. It never occurred to Ramon to think about staying together beyond the hour the desire wore off, or to seek to transform what they had into a lasting friendship. He simply was not cut from that cloth.

So when he turned the car around it had nothing to do with emotions he might be developing for Babe, or even promises he made, privately, to Shelley. People didn't matter that much to him. What turned him around was primordial. He pounded the wheel, yelled and loop-de-looped off of the road to Mexico because of a deep inner need to live life according to his own standards of fairness, out from under the shadow of the disingenuous life patterns of Jilda and Ramon, Sr.

Two hours later, pulling in to Desert Hot Springs after ten plus years trying to escape its clutches brought an involuntary shudder into his neck and shoulders.

The Wagon Wheel Inn brought back a lot of memories, not all of them favorable. He refused to sit in his usual spot for fear of rekindling the vision of himself he held back then. Instead, he took a barrel chair at a wood table and turned his back to the bar to discourage any townie girls from joining him. His worst moments here were shaking those sloppy types loose, sometimes exacerbated when some gal pal's hunky date eyed him. He could spot a mark pretty easily and the only thing you had to worry about was one of them turning inward on himself before he got what he wanted, drunkenly advancing with self-hate deep in his eyes, shouting things like, what you lookin' at faggot, sputtering him on to fight with the thing he thirsted for.

Bar fights were normal in Desert Hot Springs so a scuffle here or there usually added up to a whole lot of nothing. You just can't back down and you've got to trust someone will hold you both away from each other. Plus, to be honest, there was always a little thrill in knowing he stirred up those emotions in men in such a way that couldn't be ignored.

But as he sat there now, he had a revelation: unlike all those years ago, his pockets were full with tens and twenties with more where that came from, and for the first time in his life, there wasn't a thing anyone could offer him that he didn't have already. His gratitude towards Shelley increased exponentially in that moment. Without the deal they made together, how could he have ever said that to himself? He was happy, sitting there drinking his *cerveza* pint, dreaming of the day the three of them would come together to finish what Shelley set in motion. He felt bad for Babe, that it had to end the way she said, but if Ramon felt any debt it was to her, not him.

TWELVE

"**Y**ou're rubbing salt in his wounds when you should be applying bandages." Which Shakespeare play was that from, Shelley tried to remember. She guessed it was *The Tempest* but when you haven't read them in a while, they blend in your mind.

Anyway, it would work, she was pretty sure. Granules of Morton's salt on Manny's tongue would get his saliva flowing and would dissolve without any trace. If he swallowed fast down the wrong pipe, in his condition, as the doc said in so many words, it would all go into his lungs. Pretty much a 50-50 chance of success and right about now she liked those odds. Death by salt. It almost made her laugh, but she held it in so no guard would come checking on her again.

It's very hard to be alone and not talk to yourself at all. Or even talk to dumb old Manny, laying there, eyes open, like some kind of bullfrog. When she had the dog, she talked to her all the time. They had conversations back and forth, though Shelley filled in both sides. Ack, god, the dog. A wave of grief struck, her body failed for a moment, and she collapsed in a chair. This time she dared not say it aloud but again she thought, how did I get here?

"I wasted time and time doth now waste me."
Richard the Second, for sure. She was glad that play
came to mind because she liked the plot. The weak
king dies. The new stronger maybe Machiavellian
monarch takes his place. Yes, that's how she got here.
She orchestrated it. She accepted her position under
Manny to overthrow him. She planned to win, not to
lose. This bump in the road, this detour of fate with
Manny the Bullfrog staring at her now, brainless, just
required an act of bravery on her part. She had to rise
to the occasion. Time would not waste her. She was
the incoming, not the outgoing.

When they would eventually surround him, finally
dead, would anyone care that he was gone? Would the
doctor he kept on staff, the goons, the drivers, the
money people who may or may not have done well on
their investments, the growers and the laborers, the
office staff — outside of needing new employment,
would any of them care?

You know who would? The damn children's
hospital bureaucrats who all get to keep their jobs
with their new marijuana-money endowment. The
lawyers, they'll all be there, with those trite looks of
practiced empathy. I'm so sorry for your loss.

She didn't even think she'd have to cry. Everyone
would just imagine standing in her shoes, so much
tragedy, so quickly: she's in shock, the poor girl, they
would think. They'd avoid eye contact for fear of

catching, by osmosis, whatever curse had befallen her
to bring her this mountain of grief. Hand over mouth,
again she stifled a laugh. This one scared her: was she
losing her mind just a little? Was this becoming too
much to bear without a single ally at her side?

What if those two bastards ran? Time was against
her, sitting here, when she needed to be headed
there, to Palm Springs, to keep Frank aligned. And
why did she worry more about Frank's loyalty than
about Ramon's? In the end, they were both strangers
to her, not to be trusted, and yet to pull this off she
had to quite literally hand over to them everything
that belonged to her. But how do we come to know
anyone? Isn't everyone a stranger? We meet people
all the time, we become friends, best friends, lovers,
somewhere along the line we maybe even marry one
of them.

Such a weird word: marry. Like pouring two
ketchup bottles together or combining sound and
picture, we blend with some other entity and we
become one, at least on paper. Somehow that one
you marry is supposed to be the person you think you
know best, but why? What makes someone you met
in a nightclub or a study group or at a friend's dinner
party, that you decide to open your legs and heart to,
any less of a stranger than that guy at the next table
you haven't yet met? Why do people go on reality

shows to find a mate? Because damn it if they don't find one! That's why. So, is a soul mate so randomly encountered that they might be one of fifty contestants? Or the person who sat next to you in math class? Is love really as cheaply earned as just being in the right chair at the right time? Maybe so, she thought to herself. And if so, isn't it just as valid to decide to be free of that person, forever?

If who people are doesn't really matter, and therefore you can't possibly really matter to them either, what difference does any of it make? Because if we're all just a bunch of random reality TV show bachelors and bachelorettes, expendable as soon as the next season rolls around, then none of us exist to each other beyond any given person's desire to cheat the game, in the moment, until the game dictates the bachelor has to choose only one of the finalists and surprise! Your prince charming picks the other girl.

But, so what if you lose? Why not come back on the show next season and be the one picking from the litter of wannabes? When the time came, could she choose right, between Frank and Ramon, and win the game? It's not Shakespeare but it's Shakespearean. Being a survivor all your life makes you dangerous inside. Kill or be killed, right?

She shook herself and let all of those thoughts go. She couldn't think about Frank and Ramon now. Because right now, she had to ask herself: could she dive deeper still, to find the next level of darkness, inside? This is the elimination round.

Sodium chloride. That was the only thing to think about.

THIRTEEN

Yes, the Gods wanted them to be together, Babe thought, when he came out of his room around midnight and saw Ramon's little black car in the parking lot. Babe was a Hellenist, so when he invoked the Gods instead of God, he meant it. The idea that modern man has reduced the concept of spiritual guidance from a multiplicitous smorgasbord of uniquely powerful deities down to a single judgmental white man with flowing robes sitting on a bed of clouds irked him to no end. There is no word of God. There has never been a word of God. Only words of men pretending to speak for a god. And that's a big difference.

Ramon's car was a Japanese economy number, but he honestly could not recall if it was a Subaru or a Toyota or a fucking Kia for that matter. Seeing it made his heart skip. It had the indentation above the wheel well they caused one time when they had sex on top of it in the back alley behind the Cinema Bar, so it was his. But what was he supposed to do, knock on doors? Four cars, two floors, eighteen rooms. He couldn't ask the desk clerk. He didn't smoke so he couldn't just kind of do that hanging about people do when they're having a fag. It was smart he put his car around the corner or Ramon might have decided to be more on the up and up than he wanted to be, and checked in elsewhere.

Now what, oh great rulers of the universe? If Babe goes in his room, he's gone, locked away. No chance. If he hangs around, he can be seen loitering. Or worse, Ramon somehow sees him and is unhappy about it, and then what if they get into a fight? And people bend their necks out, listening. This whole thing is wrong-headed. Why is it you can get this far and then realize you didn't think out the last bits? He ought to go to the Palm Springs house and forget it. Hide out. He ought to put Ramon out of his mind. He ought not be thinking about what he is thinking about.

Blame Aphrodite, because just then a dove startled up in front of him (or was it a pigeon) and Ramon's form—dark, silhouetted against the street lights from the main road—appeared at the end of the block, turning the corner, walking towards the hotel. Unmistakable. At this point, the hour was late for the desert. No one was out. Ramon's boots clicked on the asphalt. All the way up the drive. No other movement, no other sound. Just him, approaching, nearing, coming clearly into view.

Ramon didn't pause or make even the slightest hesitation. He just walked straight ahead, up the stairs towards Babe's room, crossed behind his back without so much as a head nod, pushed the cracked door open and went inside. It happened so quickly, so naturally, that even if you saw it, you wouldn't be sure. Babe noted the professionalism of his clandestine behavior. Ramon's been on the wrong side of the law before, he thought, and this was of course Babe's first time.

He wasn't sure of his own timing in return. Quick inside? Hang about? He play-acted putting out a cigarette (for who?), tossing nothing on the ground, turning his foot on the invisible butt, and then leaned over the railing for a gulp of night air—something he desperately needed about now. Nonchalantly (or was it stiff and awkward?), he straightened up, stretched his arms, his back, and went in. *Que sera, sera*, he thought to himself. Here we go.

Ramon was already on the bed, fully dressed, boots still on even, and curled up facing away from the door. Babe came in behind him, locking his knees into the bend of Ramon's legs, digging his chin into his shoulder. No response. He put his hand on Ramon's waist, but still no movement. Ramon reached back, grabbed his hand and pulled it around his waist. Then the Latin lover, the lothario, the hard-edged loner who needs no one and asks for nothing—he gasped and started to sob. But Babe didn't cry along with this wounded bird.

He held Ramon close. He wanted Ramon to know he was there for the right reasons, not to check on the money, not to question his loyalty, but because he couldn't stay away. They didn't need words tonight, nor did they have the energy to engage in the restless interchanging of bodily engagement. After all they had each been through to get here, after what they had done together to arrive in this place, they needed a rest from all of those human instincts. They lay there, zig zagged, and if not simultaneously, then one right after the other, they fell asleep.

FOURTEEN

When you are going to murder your husband, you take your time. You pace. You wring your hands. You ask medical what-if questions to bring everyone surrounding you around to the idea that you are imagining methods of survival, not death. You hold damp cloths on his forehead. You get caught emptying the bed pan so the night nurse can tell you that's his job, not yours.

Shelley has been the smartest person in the room since she was nine years old, when her mother died. Her father didn't hate kids, but he sure hated her. Up until the divorce, he openly favored the only kid he had wanted and the only one he would ask to share joint custody over, her older brother, Byron, the one who would come home with cheerleaders, be the prom king, play football. Can you imagine being named after rival poets? That's something you do when you have two cats, not two children. Believe it or not, no one in school ever asked them about it, not even once.

The thing about growing up where she did in Georgia is that no one wants you to be smart. They want you to be fun. If you're smart and fun, okay, fine. Entertain us! Tell wicked stories, make us howl. Do it with a drink in your hand, starting at thirteen years old even, stealing your stepfather's plum wine. Do it all through middle school and win Class Clown. But when you start to know it, when you start to feel your superiority, your exceptionalism, you're a danger. Add boyfriends into it around sixteen and no one knows what to do with you. And what if you're from the wrong side of tracks? Actually. The town had train tracks, separating the poor from the rich, up on the hill. On the hill! They were above you, figuratively and literally. You were supposed to know it, meaning, do not have intercourse with their sons. Here's a wicked story no one wants to hear: women like sex. They also like the color blue. And sports. But the minute you come out of the womb, born a girl, the whole culture gangs up and starts to stamp you with pink blankets and pretty dolls, and they teach you to withhold yourself from men.

She read somewhere once that sexually active girls almost all come from abusive home environments. What a riot. Her "real" dad left when she was in kindergarten. Her mother got remarried again, quick. Too quick. And her poor 85-IQ stepfather, Buddy, never laid an unwanted hand on her. He was scared to death of her, was more like it. When she wasn't home, he'd go into her room and look at all her books. She caught him in there once when she was in middle school, staring at them. You scare me, Shelley, because you know more than me, he'd said, and you always will. She was thirteen.

She pulled the simplest book off the shelf she could think of and handed it to him: *Catcher in The Rye*. Every teenage boy reads that tripe and then calls it his favorite book until he dies. Something about the overall cynicism and how it meets up with the final imagery of hope with him watching his sister riding a carousel. Like, it's okay to be an asshole as long as you appreciate the little things in life. Men love that story, no matter what form it comes in, so she thought even her well-meaning but wicked-slow stepfather might be able to grasp it.

He took it with him out of the room, a befuddled look on his face and she found it years later after he passed, by his bed, with whiskey rings, coffee cup stains and dust on it.

She realized then, as often as he'd been in hers, she'd never been in his bedroom before, at least not since her mother was gone, but she was packing all of his things up that weekend. It's amazing how worthless a life can seem when it is over and you are going through a person's belongings. She sent most of the garbage to Goodwill, sold a bit of furniture online and got $105,000 for their doublewide, which the real estate broker told her was more for the land than the structure.

She split that money with Byron, who had moved away with some pretty girl to have children. He never once came to the house to help her, not when Buddy was sick and certainly not once there was work to do packing up and prepping the house. In the lawyer's office to collect checks, they shook hands when they said goodbye. Byron knew she was leaving town, likely for good, and she had never bothered to record his address or phone, figuring Buddy had it, but neither one of them asked for the other one's contact info. She could no doubt find him if she wanted to, but he somehow inherited Buddy's intellect, either by assimilation or by example, so he'd be hard pressed to locate her.

Anyway, that was that. Twenty years old and she was on her own. She took the money and moved to California and paid top out-of-state dollar for her useless UCLA education. When she graduated high school, she was Valedictorian and won Most Likely to Succeed, which she always thought was awarded to her by her peers with a wink since they all knew she was a slut. Her word, not theirs. Anything for a laugh, right?

After college, she banged around Hollywood for a few years, moving her way up in the industry, first as a copy writer, then a script reader, a D-girl, and finally as an exec in charge of nothing at a company that didn't ever make a film. That's where she met Manny.

He was a potential investor in some B-picture that, if it got made, was sure to go straight to video. It was slated to star Dolph Lundgren and Brigitte

Nielsen. They were dating, maybe? Or maybe they had just been in a movie together once upon a time. Anyway, both of them were long past their prime. It was one of those projects they say will be big with European sales, and it was doomed. She was assigned the meeting with Manny, who threw the script on the desk, said it was trash and asked her out on a date instead.

It was the wild wild west and the gold rush all rolled into one big fat joint when California legalized the use of medical marijuana. That was the way Manny described it to her, as he lit a cigar with a hundred-dollar bill for dramatic effect. He had taken her to the Chateau Marmont for dinner, and they have that outside restaurant, so the cigar was allowed. But the busboy had to ask him to put out the flame the money was causing. Manny was corny and brash like that, and it was part of what attracted her to him. Of course he paid in cash too, and plunked down some wad of bills to cover "whatever" when they took a room.

The next morning in bed he explained why he had so much cash all the time. She thought she'd never see him again, but the sex was fun and he liked that she could quote poetry without needing a book. They planned a second hotel date, this time at the Four Seasons, and then they kept doing it, from the Peninsula to the Beverly Wilshire—or was it the Beverly

Hilton. The Merv Griffin one. Ah, who knows, they probably did both.

By Christmas, he had no other girlfriends, just her, and she had seen the inside of every penthouse and presidential suite L.A. had to offer. They were celebrating the holidays at the beautiful art deco Sunset Tower where Bugsy Siegel, once upon a time, had a secret apartment. When they went to the valet to check out and go their separate ways, the white Rolls that showed up had her name on the registration. The key was tied with a ribbon to an engagement ring from Harry Winston's. In the end, her classmates were right on both counts: a simple little sex date led to her being most likely to succeed, at least by their measure, because money equals happiness when you don't have any.

When the Golden State legalized recreational pot usage—this was after they were married—the floodgates opened on his business and that meant she could take baths in champagne, if she wanted to wake up with a urinary infection. That's the trouble with excess. People do things that make no sense. She was not foolish enough to waste liquor in the bathtub. What she did was drink it. A lot of it.

In the beginning she blamed herself. She felt bored and that made her weak. Go from having nothing in life to having whatever you want, and you don't handle it well, was what she told herself. But he encouraged it. He liked her being a caged bird. No friends, no work, no goals, nothing to do. Just "be," he would tell her when she got sour on it, and asked in that accusatory tone, what am I supposed to do all day? You can just "be" for a year or two—but by five years into it, you cease to exist.

That's when she got the dog. It was a stray like her, she liked to say, and when she named it Daisy, she pictured the character from *The Great Gatsby*, trapped by her own shallow nature, reveling in all that opulence. And of course it was a veiled indictment of Manny, paralleling their lives to that of a conceited and cuckolded bootlegger. She thought about naming the dog Ginevra after the woman who inspired Fitzgerald to write Daisy, but it was too esoteric even for her taste. It wasn't like Manny was ever going to get it that the dog's name let her laugh at him in front of his face—he just thought it was a normal canine moniker and a cute thing to call a pitbull. The number of times a day she got to say Daisy, picturing Mia Farrow in a floppy hat, made her happy inside. And she needed that because happiness had all but disappeared otherwise.

The simple truth: he'd grown tired of her, and she of him. Drinking made it worse, but it gave shape to the day. Well, it did if you could hold it off until the evening. She made deals with herself: no drinking until after the night time dog walk. She'd pour the first one the second she got back inside the house, even before she fed Daisy. It gave shape to the day.

Manny was never home, and when he was they fought anyway. So she'd pour another one or two, or four. Shape to the day getting blurrier. By now, she blamed him. If he didn't like her, why not just give her a wad of bills in a suitcase and send her on her way?

Maybe he would have, had she not become so indispensable. She had an important job in his organization. For one day a month she carried the bulk of the cash to storage then helped Manny bury what they'd skimmed. Hauling and digging day, is what she called it. Once a month, on the last day of the month, every month. One day out of thirty, or thirty-one, like the poem from childhood: *Thirty days hath September.* You know the rest.

The rest. The rest was a slow, painful, semi-drunken measuring of days that fuzzed into one another and onward, bleary, into so many endless years. She had become an expert. She'd quote her favorite Shelley epistle "Time," verbatim from memory to Manny, and he would laugh and laugh at her pumped-up olde-tyme English delivery. She knew many of Shelley's works by heart. Still, she'd never grown out of the thrill of making her audience convulse from a belly laugh. Was the text funny? No. It was in the delivery. So play it up she would:

Unfathomable Sea! whose waves are years,

Ocean of Time, whose waters of deep woe

Are brackish with the salt of human tears!

Thou shoreless flood, which in thy ebb and flow

Claspest the limits of mortality!

And sick of prey, yet howling on for more,

Vomitest thy wrecks on its inhospitable shore;

Treacherous in calm, and terrible in storm,

Who shall put forth on thee,

Unfathomable Sea?

"Vomitest" was the thing that sent him over the edge, the way she drew it out into what seemed like too many syllables for the word, though he'd start to chortle the minute she started with "sick of prey" because he knew it was coming.

On the outside, she was a teenage girl too smart for her own good, drunk on sickly sweet wine, orating in ridiculous pomposity to get a howl or a guffaw. Inside, she meant every word. Time was killing her, in those years she spent as Manny's mule.

Now here was Time, doing it all over again. How long did she need to wait, to make this thing she was about to do seem fast enough for her but not too fast for the others who were watching her? She looked at the salt shaker she had put up high on the shelf after eating hard boiled eggs for lunch last week. Talk about measuring time. Cook a hard-boiled egg and see if it doesn't get you to thinking about the ticking of a clock. Now that's funny, she thought. The eternity of time measured by waiting for water to simmer just right, so you can make hard-boiled eggs. The very symbol of life, hardened by time, at just the exact correct temperature. There was a good joke in there somewhere.

No need. Manny was certainly not laughing now. He was gurgling, maybe. And taunting her still, from his sedentary purgatory. What might he be thinking inside of that near-dead carcass of human form? Would he maybe finally see the light, as it were, and want her to be free? After all of this time, dedicated to stealing from everyone, her included, might he gain some perspective, however silent, before his final breath?

How did I get here?! She was pretty sure she shouted it this time, because in ran the goons.

FIFTEEN

"**S**end in the cloooowns…"

Babe sang into Ramon's ear as they slow danced in their little hideaway hotel. This was the romantic side of Ramon. He liked these moments, even if he resisted them inside. How long could it all last anyway? He may as well let himself enjoy it.

Babe woke up that morning with an idea of his own—not really a deviation from the main program but a fill-in piece that Shelley hadn't thought out. They couldn't leave Ramon's trunk full of money in a parking lot in Desert Hot Springs. Besides it's not like Ramon could just start carrying stacks of cash into his room. Even if he could, now you've got millions in a flophouse apartment which gets cleaned eventually. No matter if you hang the Do Not Disturb sign on the knob, there's no way that's safe.

Eureka! The car should be garaged, hence, why not shelter it in Palm Springs. Then, once the vehicle was there, why not Ramon too? We're talking a three-bedroom house with enclosed, off-street parking. Who'd even notice another vehicle? Meanwhile, so what if it looked like they were together, too? Palm Springs has the largest gay population per capita in the whole country, so that's no trigger. The reverse.

It's the perfect cover. They were more invisible as a couple than Babe would be on his own. Neighbors see a single man in a big house and they start getting ideas about helping him, or bringing him oranges from their fruit tree grove. A couple of men, people jump to conclusions and leave you alone unless you reach out to them. It was a better idea, and if Shelley were here, she'd agree.

Babe figured they should get up early to separate back to their rooms, but Ramon had lived here and the truth is, desert people are up at the crack of dawn, getting their exercise or walking the dog before the pavement is too hot for their paws. By 10am, the sun rises up and they're all back inside, asleep again, or watching TV, or "working" which is always in quotation marks in these parts because most people are retired or unemployed, living off welfare.

Instead, they took their time. Ramon watched Babe shower and then he hopped in as well. They hadn't been naked together since before the crime, and everything still worked the way it was supposed to. Maybe better now that Ramon wasn't holding as much back. Ramon walked the four doors down to his room unnoticed, each checked out separately, hours apart and no one batted an eye.

Lust rots, love grows. It's a lyric Babe had in his head now and, for the first time in years, he actually felt a song forming. It started when he thought about the nosey neighbors and their fruit trees. It needed more, he thought, because right now he couldn't get Nazareth's "Love Hurts" out of his mind for the melody. Plus, it sounded like the kind of phrase you might find embroidered on a pillow in a thrift store. If there were more words, he'd get off of it, like maybe, "Everybody knows, lust is a fruit that rots, love is a tree that grows." He was too old to be a pop star but maybe he could be a songwriter. He still knew some people who knew people.

This is how he was thinking—not like he was going to be on the run for the rest of his life, but more like that there would be a settle down period and then, having the means, he could maybe try his hand at something real. Anyway, instead of listening to his music like usual, driving his way to Palm Springs, he was dreaming up this new song in his head.

Maybe Shelley could help him with the words. The minute that occurred to him, he realized he hadn't given her a thought for close to twenty-four hours. His stomach sank. What if she's already at the house? What if everything went like clockwork and she got out? You think so much about things going wrong when you do something like this, you rarely think about everything going right. Only right was wrong now.

He told Ramon he'd stop at the market, load up,

park, and then leave the garage open, since he would get there first. Then Ramon could arrive close behind him, pull right in and shut it. The design of these houses was such that once you were in, no one really knew. It's part of the architect's genius, with the idea they would be vacation houses. Home or not home, from the street, the places looked the same. The perfect hideaway for a couple of thieves on the run or a couple of clandestine lovers wanting to be alone.

He hadn't turned on Shelley. Not really. He just wanted this idyll he had in his mind's eye, now. Dreams are dangerous, he knew, from years of feeling them fail. Maybe it would be better if Shelley were sitting in the living room right now, because that's where they left it. The very last look in her eye, back there, on the floor of the hallway, told him all he needed to know. They had done it, she seemed to be saying. It was a rollicking success, the whole effort. No pleading, no needing, no anger, no blame, no relief, no regret. Just a deep look of understanding, that they had achieved what they set out to do. If she were indeed there, waiting for him, still wanting him probably, maybe he should put this childish hope to have what he wanted from life on ice. Fate would decide it, not him.

Ralph's is a fantastic supermarket, and he loaded up not one but two full baskets with provisions. The directive had been to stay at the house three weeks before moving on, no matter what. So, whether the stockpile of food was for him and Ramon, or for him and Shelley and Ramon, they'd need it all. Luckily, the market is one of the last places every other person still wears masks post-vaccine, so he was perfectly anonymous at checkout, even with the *de rigueur* banter with the perky register clerk. Yes, it was a lot for one, ha-ha, but I had to get enough for you to come on over for the party after your shift, didn't I? Bring your swim suit, I'll be in the pool with a cocktail. You have a good one too.

The last turn into Kings Point is a calm one, mountains looming large in front of you and behind you, onto a smooth private road recently repaved. There's the one bump to slow you down to the posted speed limit of 10 mph, presumably because in 1969 when the place was built, people had children. Now, it's all 50+ year-old homosexuals who have remodeled and upgraded, or nonagenarian widows with vultures circling above in their real estate jackets.

Shelley's house was painted the whitest of the five shades of white allowed by the Home Owners Association, and she long ago did away with any of the Beverly Hills style hedges and plants in favor of a desert-friendly landscape to minimize the time any gardener might need to lurk about. For her, this place was always about being private, and in fact it was she who lobbied the HOA board for the entry road signs to say just that. Everyone has the same door style on their two-car garages and the CC&Rs clearly spell out that you use them and close them directly after entry so there are no cars on either Kings Road East or Kings Road West, unless you have visitors or workers on site.

When he hit the button on the remote Shelley had given him, the door rose with an electronic whisper and revealed both empty spaces. There you have it, he thought. The answer from his Gods. He left the garage open while he took the several trips he needed to unload groceries, and in that time, he felt certain not one car passed. The weather was on his side, too, as at 110 degrees, pedestrians were unthinkable. Even an active A/C was no hint of occupancy as everyone in the area knows to leave theirs set at 88 degrees to protect their artwork.

Always be ready with a story, Shelley had taught him, so he put his mask back on, and "accidentally" forgot to push the garage button that lowered the door as he went inside for the last time. If a helpful soul knocked to let him know he was momentarily in violation of the rules, he'd point at his mask and say he was just back from the store. Most likely Ramon would pull in any minute, shut the garage door behind him, and they'd be set.

For how long was anyone's guess, since there were no phone calls allowed. If Shelley had complications, they would wait out the three weeks. Any worse than that, she said she wanted them to get on with life without her. Imagine her dead. Or worse, alive and caught. In either scenario, the money was theirs to split. He wished her no ill will, but should that be how this plays out? Babe was not thinking of a splitting of the money. And neither, quite honestly, was Ramon.

SIXTEEN

Ramon felt uneasy. He checked the trunk before he left to make sure everything was still there, and of course it was. Why would anyone break into a banged up heap like his—he even left the windows down to telegraph the owner had nothing inside to steal. It's a trick you learn living in the ghetto. People who lock things have something to lose, people who don't, don't—but Desert Hot Springs is Desert Hot Springs, where some *pendejo* might risk going to jail to sell off the spare tire in your trunk for five bucks.

Internally, he was glad Babe broke the rules and found him. A long weekend in that town was going to be a lot, and if it turned out to be the full three weeks? Hell. He agreed the car would be safer enclosed. Still, he knew he was playing with fire.

Entry went as planned, and playing house was fun. Ramon had given Babe the shopping list and he cooked. So while there was nothing to do but wait, they ate, they drank, they swam, they sunned, they made love, and they talked. Well, Babe talked. A lot. Ramon was a good listener. His mother taught him you learn more listening than you do talking—and as she often said herself, she could charm the last drink of water off a dying man in the desert, so she would know.

Ramon's curiosity about the professor was growing. When all you're doing is having sex, you really don't care to know much about a person. Being together night and day, he started asking all those questions a normal person might ask on a first date: where are you from, where did you grow up, when did you start singing, what were your parents like?

Most of it was chit chat: Babe was born at UCLA hospital and he grew up in the foothills underneath the Hollywood sign. He started singing in the 8th grade, to audition for a school play. He won the part and everyone from there on out told him he could sing, like, for real. Some kind of star. His parents were his mother and his awful stepfather, two young professionals who both worked, and as far as he could tell, cared more about all of that than they did about raising kids. They fought more than they conversed. He broke plates she cared about, she painted walls orange to irk him. They almost never sat down for family dinners, thank the Gods, because when they did, it tended to end in tears.

Did they support you or stand in your way? That last one really set him off. They both pretty much left him to his own devices, which taught him life's most vital survival skill—sink or swim. His stepfather quite literally banged that lesson into him one summer, when they went camping by a lake. To teach young Babe to swim, the bastard threw him into the water, over and over again while his mother stood and watched.

At high school graduation? He was tapped to sing the class song: from the movie *Fame*, "Out Here On My Own," of which the irony was not lost on him. It was at the Hollywood Bowl which was a school tradition. At one point in the tedious ceremony, he watched his parents get up and leave early, right after he crossed the stage for his diploma, but before his song or his award, and when he asked them why they left instead of meeting him backstage at the end of the pageantry like all the other families, his mother said it was to avoid getting stuck in traffic. The Hollywood Bowl has stack parking, she reminded him, and if you don't get out it can be a nightmare.

In college, he won every award they gave to an undergrad at NYU except for the one for Song Composition which went to another kid, and when he walked out of the ceremony with his mother and her then-boyfriend, she said, "Well, it's too bad you're not a writer."

Or how about when he was twenty-three, and the first time he told his mother he was in love, with a beautiful young man named Joe. Instead of rejoicing in his growing manhood, she cried, because she would never have grandchildren. This is a woman who marched on Washington for civil rights.

Or how about the time he was raped at 10 years old, walking from Cheremoya Avenue Elementary School to meet his older cousin several miles away at LeConte Jr High, with not quite enough money in his pocket to buy the magic tricks he wanted at the toy store on Hollywood Blvd. A gangly twenty-something-year-old street kid preyed on Babe's desire to make a few extra last-minute bucks, and lured him away from Bronson Avenue, into a side alley, saying he could make several dollars wrapping candy at his friend's place. He ended up face down with his pants around his ankles on a dirty mattress in a hidden cove next to the Argyle off-ramp of the 101. Maybe the kid let him go, maybe Babe ran at just the right moment. Instead of going to the toy shop, he walked home, all the way up Beachwood, and knocked on the door of his mother's office to tell her what had happened. She was a psychologist, working at home, and the rule was that you never interrupted her while she was in session. Never. Even though he must have looked like he had seen a ghost, and even though his face was streaked with tears and he likely couldn't form a sentence, she told him she'd be up to see him during her next ten-minute break between clients. When he was finally able to tell her, the family decision between her and her then-husband was that involving the police would be too harmful for the boy. Maybe that was a good decision. Or maybe they all let a serial rapist wander the streets to abuse another victim another day.

For as long as he could remember, his mother had told a story about her lost dollhouse. His grandmother had packed up their home to move the family from Michigan to who knows where for a better life. When they unpacked on the other side, his mother's dollhouse was missing. She was told that they had to sell it, and it pretty much became his mother's Rosebud, the symbol of everything that haunted her from childhood into the misery of her adulthood. The more he's grown up, the more Babe's come to realize: to her one, he has a thousand dollhouses. A thousand dollhouses. It could be the name of his autobiography. Maybe he'd put it on his tombstone. Here lies Babe. He died of a thousand dollhouses.

Ramon stayed mostly silent through all of it, still feeling no reason to give away the keys to his own store. Babe asked questions but he hemmed and hawed and avoided any real admissions. Over the years with all the men he'd been with—and there had been hundreds—he learned the mystery only made him more attractive. Like those strong silent types in movies everyone falls for even though all they do is grunt and shrug and spit sideways onto the ground. Clint Eastwood. Steve McQueen. Paul Newman. Lee Marvin. It was an American ideal he'd learned by watching old movies on TV to learn English as a kid. Maybe it's part of why he knew so few words when he first started his hustle in Desert Hot Springs.

As they hung out like this, talking and not talking, days quickly became a week, and into the second week, Ramon began to really wonder what he should do.

SEVENTEEN

For most of life's important choices, there is no perfect moment: when to confess you're having an affair so you can tell your girlfriend you're leaving her; when to spend the rainy day money and buy a new car you don't really need; when to tell your boss at the supermarket to shove it so you can change jobs even though you've got nowhere to go; when to kill your husband who's been laying in a coma for close to two weeks.

Today was the day, Shelley had decided when she woke up. The groundwork had been laid and he had lain in bed long enough. He will finally have been layed out to rest soon after she did lay the salt lightly upon his tongue. She was making herself laugh, inside, with all the variations on that one. You begin to see how much fun her beloved Shakespeare must have been having, killing off kings and other fools with the English language.

Up and about, she dressed as usual in this fully unusual situation, and went down for breakfast, which she tended to make by herself and eat alone, even though there were several other people now, lurking about the house. When she reached out to spice her eggs the way she likes them and found only pepper, well, that's when she started, from the blackness of her soul, singing in her head, the suddenly mirthful part about that lost salt shaker from "Margaritaville," i.e. one of the worst songs ever, to help her through what was sure to be a tough day. Why was everything suddenly so funny, she wondered? If she learned anything from being around Frank, it was that there is a perfect lyric to fit any situation.

The whole abnormal day could not have begun more normally. Handsome Goon Number One, as she had taken to calling him, took most night shifts watching over Manny while she was sleeping, so he was the one she relieved this morning too. He lingered as was the norm, to talk a bit, to commiserate, to offer sympathy. Attention from such a looker made her feel good. So what? The staff could only view her as a dedicated wife at this point, the routine was being met, the honorable thing was being done, the obligation was on display. The only variable that remained was whether or not Manny would jolt awake one day, or slide off into the abyss, going gentle into that good night, or would he continue to rage, rage against the dying of the light.

This was how her head was working right now, in a jumble of quotes and phrases and lyrics and word games. The categories are: Shakespeare, Dylan Thomas, Bad Music of the 1970s. Yep, left to this much longer, she might soon be playing mind-Jeopardy against me, myself, and I. Her eyes must have been darting around, or something, because as she watched Handsome Goon Number One close the door, she had to meet his sympathetic last gaze back at her, so she shot him a telepathic defense: You try holding every real thought you might have inside for days on end, pretending to be someone you're not, see if you don't go a little mad. The door clicked closed and she took a deep breath.

And then the damn song popped back in her head, but this time about how people blame the woman when it's really the man's own damn fault for bringing life's unhappiness down upon himself via his decades of lousy behavior. Hilarious. She patted Manny's hand. Another deep breath. Two hours, she decided, was the right amount to let tick by, post-breakfast, before she made her move. If she let that Jimmy Buffet garbage take over any further, and for that long, she truly would lose her mind, so she tried to focus on something else. Like…how about…her Pulitzer Prize winning book idea, the one she would probably never sit down to write but if she did it would be earth-shatteringly good and win her world-wide respect and admiration.

It goes something like this: what if the history of mankind parallels the individual path of life? She had done no real research to back it up, but intuitively she felt she could prove that the human qualities of Erik

Eriksen's famous eight stages of man—from being a baby to being a toddler to being in preschool to being in elementary school to being an adolescent to being a young adult to being middle-aged to being in old age—directly line up with the evolution of societal behavior throughout the various eras and epochs of mankind.

To make the whole thing work, though, she would add one more stage to it which is pre-birth, in that the embryonic evolution of a baby inside a mother's womb is easily likened to the miraculous evolution of the start of man—sludge, rising out of that proverbial murky lake and bit by bit forming into something resembling a human-to-be. Once you can visualize that, then it follows that the Stone Age epoch of the caveman is akin to being a baby. Simply put, goo goo gaga equals unga bunga. Then we encounter the cognitive development of language and gestures that hold meaning in order to get what you want. Food and survival are the guiding principles, and you see only as far as what is in front of you to get through the day—nothing more, nothing less. In the Bronze Age humans enter the terrible twos—inventing the wheel like toddlers build with blocks, all the while warring with everyone and anything and simultaneously envisioning the first civilizations, in Mesopotamia and ancient Egypt, forging their first attempts at getting along for the greater good. See how it lines up?

By elementary school, we're the Greeks and the Romans and we're engaged in moving beyond all of the most primitive of human instincts to start a lifelong journey of better understanding democracy, philosophy, mathematics, drama, and poetry. We're introduced to a series of systems of rules, rights and wrongs, and we already begin to struggle with success and failure on the grand scale of whether or not we will triumph over our peers or perish in a sea of mediocrity.

Adolescence is the Middle Ages, murky and dark and messy, filled with sex and disease, as we align or rebel against an overarching system that is trying, by guilt or by guidance, against all odds, to reign in our best and our worst impulses. That we survive it is a miracle, and the reward is our Renaissance into young adulthood, where depending on how damaged or enlightened, poor or rich, privileged or deprived that we and our clan have become after so much struggle, we seize, squander or envy the opportunities that abound.

And then comes adulthood, the Modern Era, that begins with the industrial revolution and marches on through to the age of information. We go to work. We forge our way against the odds or with them. We take advantage or get taken advantage of, we pollute and we build, and we embrace or reject everything we've learned so far. We make skyscrapers and we level forests. We ravage cultures and we build bridges. We are a massive contradiction of selfish progress and empathetic charity. We do daily battle against good and in favor of evil, and vice versa, within ourselves and in the outside world.

What she couldn't imagine is where it goes from here. We are no doubt headed towards the final stages of Old Age, with diminishing resources, a body Earth that is splintering and falling apart either slower or faster depending on what precautions we might now take in our collective and comparative youth. And there remains the outside possibility we somehow develop technology or maybe merge with it in the Synchronicity, to extend life indefinitely because that's how based in the Survival of the Fittest we began and the ethic to which we will always return.

There were bound to be a million holes in the argument, but if she worded it all strongly enough and backed it up with literary evidence, who would really attack it since it was such a unique idea. Even if it didn't make total sense or hold real water, it would be revered for being so bold.

Now, what does one wear to the awards ceremony when receiving the Pulitzer? Maybe Lily Pulitzer. And there she was, back on word games.

She looked at the clock and all of that thinking had killed only an hour, but it seemed good enough for her. Why wait any longer. An hour, two hours since breakfast. It was arbitrary. What difference could it make?

She edged the salt down from the top shelf, put plenty of granules loosely all over her very dry hand so they would sprinkle easily, and slipped the shaker carefully upright into her purse before zipping it shut, so it could not possibly be in sight when everyone came rushing in. She crossed over to Manny's bed, slowly, so as not to spill any traces from her palm to be discovered by forensics later, opened his mouth with her other hand, did the deed, quite expertly and happily without incident.

Manny made a sour face which surprised her as he had been mostly expressionless for the fortnight, and in only a few moments began to salivate first and then cough, violently.

For about 30 minutes it was mayhem. Anytime anyone asked her anything she just shook her head in terror. No, she had no idea what started it. No, she didn't see anything out of the ordinary. Yes, he seemed fine when Handsome Goon Number One (aka Jeff) left this morning. No, she didn't give him any food or drink. No, no, yes, no, yes, and then a bunch of maybes and I don't knows. These were not rapid fire. The questions came in response to nothing working to stop his collapse into full on cardiac and near-pulmonary arrest. She could not have planned it any better. Because of his DNR he was neither intubated nor forced to vomit (which was apparently very dangerous in his state) and so he just sputtered a lot, until finally he went silent and still.

Was he dead? She wanted to know, but she managed to say it like a frightened little wifey-woman, and the doctor lowered his eyes to the floor when he talked to her now, as he felt positive this was finally the end. No, Manny was not dead, but he would not, in his professional opinion, survive the night.

EIGHTEEN

Ramon's specialty, *carne asada*, sizzled on the grill. The trick is in the marinade. Cilantro, olive oil, soy sauce, garlic, jalapeño, cumin, and—his mother's secret recipe—both orange *and* lime juice. Of course his parents would have stolen the flank steak from the butcher, with his father running a distraction in the front of the shop, while Jilda crept silently in the back. The oranges and limes would have been lifted from another shop. They never took too much from any one store as to be noticed. In and out quick, with just tonight's dinner and maybe tomorrow's, switching positions, changing the game so you can hit the same mark more than once, sometimes up to four or five times in the month you park in a town. Then you travel on before anyone really catches on to you.

Ramon liked the idea this meat was bought, with cash, but he kept the blinders on when it came to thinking about how honestly the money had been earned. The truth is that the industrial meat complex in America is heinous anyway, so why not buy meat with stolen cash? How is it possible to have this much steak and that many chickens, in every store across the country, at all hours, seven days a week, 365 days a year? No store ever runs out. "So sorry, we're out of boneless chicken breasts this week." No. Never.

Top it with guacamole and serve with warm torti-llas. Margaritas made from fresh lime juice, orange juice, tequila and Grand Marnier.

While Ramon prepped and cooked, Babe swam laps. Johnny Mathis was now "their music" and so he crooned on the stereo more often than anyone else, playing through the outdoor speakers by the pool, in the shape of rocks. Babe had also discovered another bonus to this over-designed vacation home: the underwater speaker. You can hear the music when you swim!

Ramon was getting used to Babe's record collec-tion. He thought it pretty corny at first, all of the old school vocalists. He still liked to hear Babe's voice in his ear, but to listen to the music on its own? He teased Babe, calling it an acquired taste. Acquired how, Babe would ask, by understanding the differ-ence between good and bad? Just what kind of crap did Ramon like, anyway? Lana del Rey? That baffled Ramon. He didn't even know who that was. But it became their inside joke. Let's put on some Lana del Rey for once, Ramon would say, and Babe would roll his eyes.

Up out of the pool and straight to the patio dinner table, wet. Ramon fed him a taste of a freshly made slice of the steak. Fucking delicious. This was the life. Better, life itself. Is it possible to leave everything else behind, Babe wondered, a line, drawn in the air, that puts all that came before this moment away, behind that barrier, never to return? It was on the heels of that thought, maybe even during it, that the house phone rang and both of them froze.

Twelve rings. It felt like an eternity. Not a single thought went towards the possibility of answering, but the range of possibilities was staggering. Their voices dropped to a whisper. Was it a warning or was it someone who was on to them? Was it a wrong number or maybe a marketing call? Shelley? Manny? When it stopped, there was a pause. A moment of relief.

But then it rang again. Twelve more times.

They didn't know how to check the voice mail, and even if they could, was that trackable? Of course it was.

A Pause.

Again. Twelve rings.

You could have sliced the space between them with a dull knife. Neither one of them knew what to do and so what they did was nothing. Silent gestures replaced the laughter as they waited to see if it would ring again.

Nothing.

Only now it felt like the pinking sky was listening. Now it felt like the bats behind the palm fronds had eyes trained on them. A quiet rained down. They packed up their dinner and went inside. They closed the blinds.

No more ringing.

Before the food got cold and the ice melted in the drinks, they ate, but without any of the joy that would have been there just minutes ago.

Ramon pushed his plate away. He'd lost his appetite.

Three times felt like a code to him. To Babe, it seemed like a robo-call. Who calls three times for anything? This house has been locked up for months and Shelley said when she did use it, it was for a weekend, max. She had no friends in Palm Springs, no one would call her.

What about Manny? Ramon's voice was barely audible, his stomach in his throat, his eyes lowered to the ground, revealing it had been on his mind. Because Manny was hurt when they left, but he wasn't dead.

Ramon raised his gaze to meet Babe's eyes. Neither of them had spoken about what happened until now. And even saying his name brought a certain terror.

For all the guys knew, he had killed her by now (or worse, as she reminded them). For some reason, it simply didn't occur to them that Manny might not have made it through. Ramon was sure he would be after them, or if not them, then he would be after Shelley. Or maybe he didn't let her go.

It had been two full weeks. One week to go.

Ramon was bringing it up, so Babe decided to ask the question that burned inside. Suddenly, though, his heart sunk down into his shoes, which was such a familiar feeling he decided to describe it to Ramon first, so he could understand that he affected him in that very same way that he felt even the very first time he stuck his neck out romantically and asked Carolyn Uchimiya, in 5th grade, if she wanted to go steady. For the record, she said yes, like so many have since, as the years and the various and nefarious love affairs have raced past, some with outcomes better than others. But they have always ended, one way or another, leaving him like he is now, alone, longing for the one that might finally stick. That last part he didn't tell Ramon, because, you know, that's not something you should say out loud until you know for certain how the other person feels. So he asked the long way instead of the short way.

Was Ramon thinking, assuming Shelley is not on her way, that they would count it all out and split the money and go their separate ways? Or would they stay together and, you know, at least temporarily, combine their, uh, fortune?

Ramon couldn't believe his ears. He involuntarily laughed out loud. Was Babe really comparing him to a 5th grade crush? Should they hold hands now and go to a movie, when they might have killed a man while stealing who-knows-how-much illegally garnered cash that a whole bunch of other *coños* could decide they wanted back now that they knew it had been pilfered?

The phone just rang thirty-six times. What's that famous expression? Ask not for whom the bell rings, because you fucking dumbass: *¡Es para ti!*

Was Babe insane? Or simply naive? And that question answered itself, as it hung there, between them.

Babe had been in love many times, but he had never truly been on the wrong side of the law before.

That, oddly, turned Ramon on, being Babe's first in something.

And that's when they began to tear at each other like nothing mattered.

The only thing Ramon didn't say during the tense conversation before they hit the bed together was that he was already promised half of the take, so however that worked out, he was fine with it.

NINETEEN

When she raised the garage door, she was, to put it mildly, surprised to see two cars, both of which she immediately recognized. She didn't like the idea of parking the Rolls in front of the house on the empty street, so she lowered the door with her remote, backed her car out, drove to the end of the road that is Kings Point—more of a wishbone really, since it had a little dead end down behind the manicured hedges where she could temporarily stash her ostentatious vehicle. Rolling her one bag like she was on a vacation, she walked back the long way, across the greenbelt, past the main public pool, and around the house that in 1969 was the first model home in this enclave of forty-four houses.

Halston Gucci Fiorucci is how she described the décor she wanted, to the designer, when Manny first bought her the place they called Her Getaway. "I'm going to Her Getaway," she would tell him, when she needed a weekend of peace. He seemed to understand sometimes a woman needs to be on her own, with no one watching, in order to otherwise spend her whole life under a microscope. So, he always let her go. And she loved it here. Her disco paradise, all silver and Lucite. A room of her own, like Doris Lessing's character in "To Room 19."

Unlike Lessing's heroine, though, no one was committing suicide here. First of all, no one had any illusions of a perfect life being shattered. Second, it wasn't a dingy little hotel room, it was a 3000-square-foot dream house, with soaring beamed ceilings, glass walls, and vintage terrazzo floors. The air conditioning was what you might call icy, and the heat, when you needed it for those dramatic drops in temperature during the quiet cold desert nights, was central. Manny never once visited or even really saw the place except for that first day, when he took her there to say it would be hers, and in her name, to use as she saw fit. Well, she was using it now. The second house on the right.

She entered without ringing the doorbell, with her key.

She saw Ramon first, barefoot, shirtless, and in a bathing suit (or were they boxers?) looking awfully comfortable for someone who wasn't supposed to be there. His eyes lit up when he saw her, but not with fear. He was genuinely happy to see her alive, and he put down his glass of wine to give her a hug. Had they ever hugged before, she wondered, while in his embrace. When they separated she gave him a look that could only mean, "What the fuck?"

He explained the issue about Desert Hot Springs and Frank—he knew that's what she still called him—feeling like the car wasn't safe. He drove up there and found him and they both came back here late that night. He's been staying in the guest room (which the boys were smart enough to make it look like he had been doing), laying low, cooking at home, drinking at home, not making phone calls, pretty much just hanging out. Which, he assured her, has worked out great, with no outside interactions whatsoever. Ramon told her they've been worried sick. Six more nights and they would have had to follow her directive and disappear. Can you imagine? But now she was here!

Frank was in the shower so Ramon went to get him. He came out all smiles as well, and the three of them stood there, in a circle, holding hands, looking at each other, somber. Shelley dropped hands first, and the other two made sure their hands did not linger.

In bed that night, her head on his chest so he couldn't gauge her reactions, she wanted to know more about the last weeks and why they decided to take such chances, but Frank's story was the exact same as Ramon's. She told him she didn't need to hold on to it, she decided to just let it go. He was relieved when she agreed that it may have been the best idea after all, since she took so long to arrive. What difference did it make now, especially since there were no repercussions? As thoroughly as she had planned things out, it remained a fact that she didn't think about the potential for her getting stuck for two weeks in L.A. while all that cash was cooking in the trunk under the sun in an unguarded parking lot. She might have solved the issue another way, but hey, what's done is done. *All's Well That Ends Well*—a play that was a damnation of humanity, she thought, rife with fairy tale logic and cynicism. And that false happy ending. You only have to read the text properly to know there is a big "IF" hanging over it all. "If she, my liege, can make me know this clearly, I'll love her dearly, ever, ever dearly." Tepid ever after, at best.

She had no answer for him about the phone calls except that she really didn't like the timing. In the morning, she decided, they should implement the rest of the steps. Get rid of Frank's car. He started to balk, saying he'd rather keep it, but she insisted. Ramon needed his, to complete his return to Mexico. They had the Rolls which was hers, free and clear. They should not have an extra car on the street, not even for the final hours while they worked all the details out.

Her solution was for him to drive his car in to a CarMax tomorrow. You get appraised, sign it over, and it's gone. They wouldn't get much and who cares. Frank should go by himself, and then taxi back to someplace within walking distance. Maybe the golf club across the street. Have lunch. Walk back. Take a stroll if need-be. Everyone walks in Palm Springs for exercise so a tourist alone on foot arouses no suspicion. Just wait until no one is on or near Kings Road, duck in, and come back quietly.

The simplest acts were seeming so complicated now, he told her. The heist itself seemed easier than this part.

Her ability to dictate had not been shaken after whatever she went through back in town, and so far, she had not been willing to talk about it beyond saying it was awful. She rolled deeper in to his chest and she dozed off, easy, and even started to snore. If she had a care in the world, she wasn't showing those cards. He stared out the window at the golf course— manicured, closed, useless—wondering how he would ever get out of this.

If she were awake and he had the nerve to ask her, she would have danced around telling him: She had a plan for that, too.

In the dining room, isolated and on the other end of the house, Ramon spent his night cleaning and counting the money. Until Shelley showed up— or failed to show up—Ramon insisted neither one of them touch it. You could say it was a display of solidarity, and honestly, she did seem to appreciate it when he told her, but really he feared any real sense of the take would inspire too much greed, by one or the other of them. Babe agreed. Keeping it abstract made it less tangible, less tempting.

Just before Frank and Shelley retired, the three of them pulled the garbage bags and duffle bags out of Ramon's trunk and dragged them across the living room and close to the place Ramon's dinner still sat half eaten. It tasted much better to him now, even cold, and in between bites, he told them both he was fine staying up to do the count. He's used to working until 2 a.m. and funnily enough the last task of the night is always to count the money. Besides, if you can't trust a bartender with your cash, who can you trust?

That impish smile of his, his teeth ripping on a piece of steak, broke out at just the right moment and the three of them shared a much needed laugh. All the tension, all the worry, all the fear spilled out onto the floor like the piles of cash, money, and *dinero*, which Ramon dumped at his feet as he said each word, complete with a bullfighter's *olé* for comic emphasis. Shelley's side hurt from how hard he made her laugh and, doubled over, she finally was able to stop herself. She stood up and held out her arms. The two guys came over and the three of them embraced.

They did it, she said. They'd won. When you are close like that, in a group hug, no one can look into anyone else's eyes, and the darting wondering wandering thoughts of each remained well concealed. Ramon pushed them all apart and shooed the couple to bed.

Babe looked back, but Ramon did not return the favor. As much as he hated his real name, it near killed him to hear Ramon call him Frank. They never needed to discuss this moment, as it was a given they couldn't reveal their entanglement. The idea, at least for Babe, was that they would get through the end game and figure out, when it was over, how to meet up. He had no idea, though, what Shelley already knew, and what was in store for him.

The stacks took up the whole table. The dirt was mostly in the bags and on the outside of the wrappers. Manny and Shelley put plastic around the piles to protect them but there was no way to keep the whole operation from smelling like earth. The crude odor transported him back to his childhood, sleeping outside or in make-shift tents. Whatever scams his parents ran, they were never big hauls. They lacked Shelley's ambition, or maybe worse, had no desire to dream larger than their petty hand-to-mouth grifting.

Now here he was, on the other side of midnight, stacking this massive amount of bills atop a designer glass table in a Palm Springs vacation estate. The bundles had been pre-organized and even labeled, so he could scan them and know around how much was there: somewhere upwards of two million, maybe approaching three. The bigger the number got, the harder it was to hold the math in his head. Part of the problem was the currency itself, ranging all over the map from singles to hundreds. For the ultimate three way split (which definitely had to be the way he did it, for show, in the morning), he decided he would have to reorganize them, more like Monopoly money, by denomination. The more even the distribution looked to the naked eye, the less any one partner might question the parity.

Several times Ramon stopped, and barefooted, snuck over the two thousand square feet of cold stone flooring to hang close to the side of the tall Hollywood doors that led into the main bedroom suite. He checked himself as he approached not to get caught in the moonlight coming through the upper windows where a shadow might get cast across the bottom of the door, and alert them that he was outside lurking, listening. For what? Not words. Sounds.

He told himself he didn't care if Shelley and "Frank" had sex, but somehow, now, it ate at him. He didn't feel jealous so much as he wanted to know. Okay, maybe he did feel pangs. It wasn't anything he was used to feeling, so back at the table, he drank it aside. *Más tequila.* Naturally, that made it worse. So back he would go, more careful than the last time, to listen. The first couple of times, he did hear their muffled voices, mostly hers, but as the night wore on, it was maybe a chortle or a snore, and by then he didn't care.

Counting and drinking might not really match, but it's how he always closed the bar. Before the sun rose, he had them all separated out, just the way he wanted it to look. Even Steven, without any need for anyone to count. One, two, three. Yours, his, mine. Goodnight and goodbye.

He needed to get the smell off and when he stepped out of the guest room shower, naked, there was Babe, in his boxers. They got each other off quickly and quietly—at this point they knew what buttons to push. Babe used a wet towel to clean the important areas and out he slipped, grabbing a glass of water from the kitchen in case he needed an excuse, and then right back to bed.

Now it was Ramon's turn to stare out into the night.

TWENTY

The car dealership was uneventful. Babe worried for a moment about the info he had to give and how it would place him in the Coachella Valley, but by this point, the hiding seemed pretty much over. People sold their cars in Palm Springs all the time. Where there were casinos, people needed cash.

You walk in the door of CarMax, take a number, fill out forms about what you are selling, and hand over your keys for an inspection. After about a twenty-minute wait, they send over a representative to take your case, give you an offer and before you know it, cut you a check. It all would have been done and done in an hour or less, had Babe's randomly-assigned used car buyer not been a veritable source of local history. He made a joke about needing the money for tonight's slot machines and boom, he couldn't shut the motherfucker up.

But what Babe learned was fascinating. The Palm Springs area, apparently, has casinos due to a very particular and strange web of treaties that led to what is commonly referred to as the Golden Checkerboard. In a deal that was made between the U.S Government and the Agua Caliente Band of Cahuilla Indians, literally, every other block in Palm Springs is owned by the tribe. The other squares of the playing field remain open to the free market, and so they began to be known as "fee land," meaning, like the rest of America, you can buy it for a fee and build on it. The real estate powers-that-be call the plots controlled by the Tribe "leased land," meaning Joe and Jane Modernism can buy their architecturally significant house on land that they pay to borrow for up to 99 years, with renewals renegotiated as needed to extend. Besides the Palm Springs golden checkerboard, large areas of land peppered throughout the valley also fall under their jurisdiction, so much so that when you are buying a house, you have to ask: is this leased land or fee land?

According to this wrinkled and weathered twelve-year sober pre-owned vehicle appraiser, decades after this treaty, when we also empowered Native Americans to open casinos—presumably to gain back their self-respect through the most heinously twisted vision of capitalism as potential savior—they took the bait and ran with it, because, really, how many turquoise bracelets can you sell on Route 66 anyway? How it made sense that Native Americans, who were slaughtered by the worst imperialist instincts of cowboys moving the country west, should be given a restorative gesture from the government that includes the right to rip off paycheck-to-paycheck schmoes hoping to turn nothing into something baffles the logical mind.

P .   D A V I D   E B E R S O L E

No doubt the reparations were not designed to end up in such a bastardized picture of justice, but leave it to America to get everything wrong, even when it is trying to do the right thing. It was at this point that the guy apologized to Babe, if he was offending him. But truth is truth, he said, right behind his beg-pardon, so if you're offended by that, well, then, next customer!

History lesson aside, Babe took solace in his exposure to the local color in that, still, no one was either taking much notice of him nor could they put the three of them together, and why would they? A music professor from UCLA, an undocumented bartender, and a pot dealer's widow. They had zero in common and no reason to know one another and by tomorrow, none of them would.

Minus, you know, the one little harmless double cross.

When they woke up side-by-side in bed earlier that morning, they'd actually had a good talk. Shelley was cool—cooler than him, really—about the idea of a separation. They'd had their fun, she said. It had its outcome. Easy come, easy go. No love lost. They didn't even have sex for old time's sake. She went into the shower and he rolled over and went back to sleep.

Or pretended to, anyway. She poked back out, casually toweling that Vitti mane of hers, and said she'd thought it over and, even though this new wrinkle meant they were each going their own way tomorrow, she still wanted him to sell his car. She decided it was best if he took the train to leave town, with his share of the take, and he felt it safest not to cause any arguments since he was overall getting his way, which is how he now ended up vehicle-free, standing on Highway 111 flagging down a cab, with a check in his hand made out to cash for $1634.00, and no more unnecessary ties to his former life, or the current one, really.

It was getting simpler and easier. He took his taxi to the golf club, ordered a breakfast burrito (that little detail was in honor of Ramon), and, of course, paid in cash for all of it. The waitress sniffed the $100 bill and laughed when he said he owned two farms, so, you know, manure. It's on everything he owns. She wanted to know what he grew and that threw him for a beat, but it's Palm Springs, so he improvised: dates! It takes manure to grow dates, who knew, she wondered aloud, and he said, you have no idea how much. Hahaha, well, hm, what do you know, that's what's so great about being a waitress, you learn something new every day. And he could picture her at parties, for years to come, telling people she once met a farmer whose money smelled of dirt who told her it takes a shitload of manure to grow dates.

He was whistling when he left the restaurant and walked to Murray Canyon Drive, when, of course, a car full of bathing beauties pulled over to check their directions, a gay couple in their seventies stopped in their tracks, walking their untrained and unruly puppy, and believe it or not, yes, a nun and a little girl were crossing the street, right in front of Kings Point.

The week or so before, when he went to the market for supplies, those hours before Ramon came, he had dubbed this the Rule Of Palm Springs. R.O.P.S for short. You pull in to the empty parking lot? Another vehicle pulls in at that exact time and vies for your same space. You need spaghetti sauce in the deserted supermarket? There's one old lady, her overflowing cart parked right in front of it all, unable to decide between Ragu and Prego. Head up to check out? Some kid is mopping up and blocking the only open register. Go to fill up the gas tank? You guessed it, a chatty Cathy and her kids are at the only pump that heads the right direction for which side your tank is on. It's uncanny. You could call it Murphy's Law but that's more about things going wrong, and this was just its own strange bad timing, a world of emptiness disrupted by inconvenience.

"R.O.P.S.," he shook his head and laughed. Shelley's prescribed walk around the block was in order. Anyway, who cares, he thought. Because like in this strange L.A. getaway city where Chronos, the ruler of time, seems to have absconded somewhere between 1950 and 1980, do minutes or hours in his life even matter anymore? When he taxis tomorrow with his little suitcase full of freedom, from the golf course up to the train station to catch the 2pm to New Orleans, while Shelley speeds off in her luxury tank to who knows where and Ramon circles around his jalopy, back to get him when he "misses" that train, and they spirit off together to Mexico, will they ever worry about a clock again? Will they ever worry again? He used to tell his students that worrying is like praying for something you don't want to happen, and even though he never took his own advice, he had decided, as of right now, he was done with that. Or at least he would be in about twenty-six hours.

When he got back to the house, unfollowed and unseen, things seemed off-kilter. All the money was gone from the table and Ramon was sweating at the brow. Shelley had decided there was no reason to wait for tomorrow, Ramon explained. She had Ramon pack everything up, and two thirds was already in his trunk. He was going to drop Frank off at the train station. Why not? It's easier. And then he could just go on his way. Her car was loaded too.

Ramon told him that the phone rang again, and when Shelley answered there was no one on the other side, or at least no one spoke, so they were spooked. She wanted the guys out of there, ASAP, and if that meant they had to drive around a bit first, she didn't care. Ramon said maybe they could go up to Joshua Tree, drive through the park before the train came, and Shelley liked that idea because it seemed normal but also isolated.

Babe's thoughts were reeling. If it was all on the up and up, on the one hand, it made his plan for him and Ramon easier. On the other hand, Shelley didn't usually just change things and if she did, she certainly didn't let someone else do her talking. So, yeah, alarm bells sounding, but there they stood, Shelley just staring at him as Ramon spoke, unreadable, implacable, and Ramon with keys in hand. Meaning all of this was happening.

Now.

TWENTY-ONE

Babe rode in silence in the passenger seat, thinking if he gave him the mind space, Ramon might decide to tell him what was actually going on. Traveling the other way—from Desert Hot Springs into Palm Springs—is a relief. Seeing the huge San Jacinto mountains loom majestic after surviving all that poverty quite literally makes your shoulders drop. Leaving Palm Springs, though, is an exercise in anxiety, as the roads narrow and the deceitful beauty of the false oasis falls away. Going north on Indian Canyon, once you cross Racquet Club Rd, the last wide boulevard of the town, you're left with the part of this big little city no one wants to think about. Still unfinished and abandonded mid-century modern condo complexes give way to liquor warehouses and auto body repair and energy plants and budget home improvement storerooms — all the out-of-sight, out-of-mind underpinnings that it takes to build and maintain a luxury lifestyle.

The final gasp of enchantment on the way to Joshua Tree is an accidental man-made wonder—the infamous and oft-photographed wind farm, with close to three thousand bright-white, slow-turning, 300-foot high NASA-built wind turbines featuring propeller-like blades each sporting a wingspan of half a football field. They not only harness the breeze and turn it into pure energy, they spark visions of a space age eternity, with their promise to power future generations long after we've abused the earth, taking all other energy she has to offer.

This should be a happy moment, Babe thought. Why was it so mired in dread? To break the silence, he broke into song, acapella.

Like a circle in a spiral

Like a wheel within a wheel

Never ending or beginning

On an ever spinning reel

Not even a smile from Ramon, so he wound up for the big finish.

As the images unwind

Like the circles that you find

In the windmills of your mind

Still silence. So they drove on, beyond the windmills, across the Interstate and onto the barren roads that lead through that town from which they each previously escaped.

Finally, Babe couldn't take it anymore so he asked.

"What the fuck is happening?"

Ramon couldn't speak, though. Not wouldn't, or didn't. Couldn't. Babe saw Ramon's brow furrow and his lips tighten, and for the first time realized that Ramon was following Shelley's directions under duress. When Ramon ran right through the stop sign at Dillon Road, he began to worry, more for this beautiful man driving, twisted inside, than for himself.

Babe told him to pull over, that they couldn't drive through stop signs like that or they might get caught. But he only drove faster. As they swung a bit wildly through the turn onto Highway 62, he told Babe to open the glove box. Why, he wanted to know, what's in there?

Just open it, Ramon said, so he did and it was what he expected to see. The gun they had used to hit Manny. It was supposed to be unloaded, but it wasn't, Ramon told him. He was driving them to a spot where he was supposed to kill Babe.

Shocked into his own silence, Babe struggled for the words to ask what had changed, and this is when the scenery really started to spin.

Nothing had changed, Ramon told him. This had been the plan since the very start. He and Shelley had been chalking out this whole thing for a year before Babe walked up to her in the sculpture garden. The beauty of their plan was that it didn't matter if the guy was straight or gay because they had both bases covered. Then, in walks the perfect guy, who hit an inside the park double.

Baseball analogies were over Babe's head, but he got the gist. They could both play him, was the idea. This next question he wasn't sure he wanted to ask, but R.O.P.S.—there was someone blocking what used to be a wide open aisle, so why not?

"Does she know about us, then?"

"Know about it? She set it up. She cut me in half because she knew I had the hardest part. At the end."

Which was, apparently, in process.

Babe felt rattled, and for more than one good reason. One, he couldn't understand why Ramon was telling him. No doubt Shelley came up with a good disposal scheme. Why not just go along with the story as is—shoot him in the back of the head and dump him over some rocks in the Monument, roll him down a big hill, or whatever Shelley told him to do, to be found some years later by some hapless hiker who ventured a new path.

A black crow, poking around roadkill by the center line, suddenly fluttered up in front of them and Ramon barreled right through it, shrieking as it thumped the windshield and gasping again when his back wheels thumped over its carcass. *Maricon!*

That's when Ramon's eye started to leak a tear, and Babe knew exactly why he was telling him. He couldn't do it.

"You can't do it, can you?"

Ramon composed himself while he drove on. No more tears.

Wait. Is half of the money in the trunk right now? Is Ramon going to take it and drive off with it after he does the deed? That seems so easy, then. They just don't do it. They skip all the extra steps they were going to have to go through, and beat it out of town.

Ramon took a breath and carefully pulled the car over. The time had come to tell this stupid idiot everything. So that's how he started, quiet.

"You're such a stupid fucking idiot."

Out it all came. Calm. No histrionics, just information. No, Shelley didn't give him the money. He is supposed to go up to Joshua Tree and kill Babe, then come back to the house where she would split the money 50/50, and he would leave for Mexico.

Ramon knew more about Shelley than anyone, because in that year she came in to the bar, during much of which she was too drunk to remember just how many of her beans she had spilled, she told him things—like, what her mother didn't protect her from that made her happy inside when the woman died, accidentally, in that fall down the stairs. Or was it an accident? What her stepfather and she kept on doing

for another long eleven years until she decided she
didn't like it anymore, which led her to learn how to
poison a man in broad daylight and get away with it.
When Ramon met Shelley, he thought maybe she'd
just had a hard life and deserved a break. Now he was
scared of her.

"So you're going to kill me because you're scared of
her?"

That question made Ramon crazy. The gun was
still sitting in front of them. Why didn't Babe think
about grabbing it to protect himself, Ramon wanted
to know. And he answered the question himself:
"Because you're a stupid idiot." Ramon grabbed the
gun and started waving it around as he spoke, a bit
like the mad person he was accusing Shelley of being.

No, Ramon had no intention of killing Babe. He
was going to put the miles on the car that proved he
took him to Joshua Tree. Then he was going to go
back and get his money, their money, and then they
were going to leave this whole thing behind them.

Babe wasn't quite sure what to do. But he knew this
much. He had no choice. He had done all of this, up
to this moment, to somehow buy himself back from
a life that had taken everything from him. It came
down to this. No choice. Doors were closing inside
of his chest, hundreds of them already padlocked, and
now that last few remaining, shut, tight.

So when Ramon said to get out of the car, he did it. And when he said to walk around to the back, he did that too.

"Look." Ramon popped the trunk as some kind of proof, to show him there was no money inside. Even as he was staring down into it, Babe wondered if he was about to be shot in the head and thrown inside. Slam, the trunk went back down and Babe involuntarily jumped and shouted out.

"Back in the car," Ramon demanded, and, captive, Babe did as he was told. They rode on in silence for close to another hour. It made Ramon furious that Babe failed so miserably to protect himself. From Shelley, from him, from all of it.

They paid at the unmanned gate, $5 for one car entry by swipe of your card, or by cash in an envelope that you slide into a plastic box. They chose the cash option, of course, and drove through the park until they reached the spot Shelley had directed Ramon to take them to.

It was a smart place to get rid of someone, Babe thought. Shelley always thought things out. No guard entry. Windy side roads. A lookout point with a huge drop behind a chain that was meant to keep tourists safe. Today was a good day to do it too, because the weather was awful. Overcast, rainy and sad, and no view, so who would be here? No one, that's who. He wondered if tomorrow was forecast for clear weather, which is why she moved it all up a day.

"Get out of the car," was the only thing Ramon said.

Informed or not, he figured this was it. He knew all about Ramon's past, but up to this moment, he never thought he himself was in bed with that hustler. He thought he was with a tangled soul, a man who needed to be set free, like he did. He thought they had a simple plan to get away together, to a simple life. Even without the money in the trunk, if it were him, and if he had any choice right now, which he knew he did not, he would say, let's go. What we have, or at least what we could have, is worth more than anything you might be given back at Shelley's house.

Did he say any of that to Ramon? Of course not. Because you don't really talk about love to a person with a gun who has point blank told you he was sent on this mission today to kill you.

They stood side by side, looking out at what amounted to nothing. A clouded over universe, that if clear, must be a sight to see. Nothing can be quite beautiful, too, he thought. A whistle of air. A shift from one gray to a darker shade. The scrape of Ramon's boot. A vastness. A click.

Oddly enough, after a lifetime of music coming into his head during important moments, all he heard now was a ringing silence. That notion brought the lyric about his old friend, darkness, and everything that brought him here to this precipice, presumably to be with him again: *"The Sounds of Silence..."*

Ramon fired.

Babe fell to his knees.

One single shot.

Out into the canyon.

TWENTY-TWO

To have the house to herself was exactly what Shelley needed, or so she thought. She flopped onto the sofa with a *Palm Springs Life* magazine but got restless within a few minutes. She opened the fridge but just stared inside it. You know when you want something but you don't know what you want, so nothing looks good?

How about outside? Fresh air, and all that nonsense. The back gate by her pool opened onto the empty golf course, closed for the summer up until Thanksgiving when more tourists returned. She took a walk across the first tee, past ducks feeding on fallen olives, to the lake, which at this point resembled more of a lagoon, green algae forming on the top without the usual motion stirred in the water via the big spurting fountain, also dormant for the off-season.

Several dead tilapia carcasses, decomposing in the heat exposing intricate skeletons and sharp white fangs, lined the edge. A heron floated out around the dry copper lily-shaped Disney Fountain, so named because Walt had it made and donated to the course, in honor of his wife Lillian. Her real estate agent told her: Most people don't know that Walt bought land in Palm Springs with the intention of creating Disneyland. Apparently, he thought better of building an outdoor amusement park in a town that reached 120 degrees in June, July and August.

What an American success story Disney is, she thought to herself. Who would imagine all your dreams could come true by drawing a cartoon mouse? Or that you could parlay that winsome rodent into a full blown empire, self-dictating to an entire nation of children and their parents, six going on seven decades' worth of harmful and insidious sexist notions of how men and women should behave. Someday my prince will come.

If life were only that easy.

The prince was a fool and now he was gone, by her own hand. Many princes have come and gone, really. Nothing happens unless you make it happen: that's been her motto since, well, since that which cannot be talked about. No waiting on fairy princesses or good queens to be allies towards protecting her from the systemic degradation of her mind and body. She might just build herself her own fucking fountain that spurts 100 feet into the air. Fuck you, Walt Disney. Take that.

And with *that*, thunder sparked and a downpour began. Hot summer rain, where the drops are so big and so far apart you don't get wet. She took temporary refuge under the olive tree waiting for it to pass, shooing the handsome green-backed drakes and their dull brown lady friends. The sight of them only enraged her all over again—the men scrambling first, the women left to fend for themselves. If she had Elmer Fudd's rifle, she'd shoot every daffy-ass one of them—the males for winning the gene pool lottery and the women for going along with it all.

Standing there, water falling from the sky all around, she was taken back to the first rain she could remember. She was six, and she and her mother had been taking a walk in the trees behind their house. It wasn't a forest exactly, more like a grove of pines, but to her child's mind, it loomed large and foreboding. It went dark and that's when the deluge began to fall on her, out of nowhere, from on high. Her first exposure to this nonsensical expression of nature, she screamed in panic to her mother, who—until now, she had not noticed—had tears streaming down her face from some unknown adult problem little Shelley had no ability to grasp. In response to her daughter's fear, her mother burst out laughing, looking like a mad woman with running mascara, her coiffure giving way and drooping off to one side. You should be scared, she told Shelley, because God is crying. She pointed up to the heavens. He's crying and it's all your fault.

Can you imagine? Her husband had left her that morning, saying he couldn't take the pressure of raising a family, and as far as her mother was concerned, Shelley was to blame. You'd think she'd have caught herself for being so horrible, and would run to the girl, scoop her up in her arms and say things like Mommy's sorry, she didn't mean it. Instead she marched over, stared down at her daughter, and slapped her, hard. In that moment, Shelley's heart turned black. Even her child's mind knew she was being wronged but what she could not know was that her battle was centuries old, so there would be no righting it.

The storm subsiding a bit, she tentatively took steps back towards the house. A gust seemingly from nowhere loosened a heavy palm tree husk and she had to dance as it fell, from close to a hundred feet, directly towards her head. She jumped to the left at the very last moment, and managed to avoid it striking her down. The rainfall had all but stopped, but the blustering weather mirrored her mood now, whipping about the landscape, swirling up the dried out sand traps. Another thunderclap and more rain. She was caught, no longer under a benign shower but inside a veritable monsoon complete with hurricane swirls and debris in the air. She was thrown down on the fairway, or was she struck by something airborne? She gathered herself and ran with the intensity of someone being chased, even though there was no one around but her.

Breathless, she rushed to the open slider on her

patio. Had she left it open? Using all her might against the wind, she whooshed it closed, turned around and stopped dead in her tracks at the sight of the man standing before her.

TWENTY-THREE

When Ramon turned onto Kings Road, he was pretty sure things would be calm. A round had been fired from his gun, the mileage was correct, and Babe was not with him. Still, he knew she was full of tricks so his index finger was trained on the trigger, his bar pistol loose by his side, as he parked inside the garage. The thing is, he was 99% sure that he was carrying the only lethal weapon. The 1% was just that Shelley variable—the fact that she was a con artist and a snake, not to be trusted. Especially now, at the final gesture of the whole she-bang: the money split.

To gain an element of surprise, even if briefly, he decided to enter through the back, going past the A/C equipment, and out to the pool area. No sign of Shelley there or at the bar inside. So many decisions made so quickly so he took a moment to take it all in. The recent rainfall made the cement smell like it was on fire. He'd never had a house this grand, he thought, and quite honestly never thought he would. He couldn't believe that this whole thing was nearly over, like the final round of a game show with real life consequences.

In his days in Desert Hot Springs, the other television program he watched religiously was *Deal or No*

Deal, the one where all the scantily clad pretty girls have silver briefcases filled with a cash value from $0.01 to $1,000,000. A perky contestant chooses one briefcase from a selection of twenty-six, trying not to eliminate the ones that represent $200,000 to the million, because those are the big prizes you want left at the end. Over the course of the game, the contestant gesticulates and jumps up and down with alternating moments of grief and glee as he or she eliminates cases from the field, periodically being presented with a "deal" from The Banker to take a cash amount and quit while ahead. It's a simple equation about the law of averages, because at some point the amounts left on the playing field dwindle, as does your offer from The Banker. Ramon would scream at the screen, telling the numbskulls to take the deal before they lost everything because this is how he thought: how much money do you need to change your life? He pondered that question a moment, and then opened a glass door to the living room.

The last thing he expected to see was Shelley in a chair, a gun pointed at her head.

Shelley's Handsome Goon Number One had found her. He spun around when Ramon entered. Gun up, eyes blazing. Greed. Desire. Fear. Ramon acted instinctively and just shot the poor sap. Dead between the eyes. Blood everywhere. A real fucking mess.

Ramon dropped his gun from the shock of it.

Even with all of his bravado, he'd never shot a person before. His parents trained him to fire a gun, in case it ever came up in a life on the wrong side of things where it was bound to, in one way or another. But now that the moment was here, it stunned him.

Shelley calmly stood up and rolled her eyes as if to say, what took you so long. She leaned down to the dead guy to check his pulse. Ramon figured, though, that was a foregone conclusion. Instead, she came up with his gun, trained now on Ramon.

The whole thing was a pretty dumb situation, really, she explained. This is Jeff, the guy who watched over her when Manny was in his coma. She tried to befriend him to her advantage, flirted a little even, but he wasn't having any of it. Somehow her behavior must have tipped him off, made him question whether or not she had all the missing buried treasure. Maybe the flirting was a bad idea.

Anyway, he was the one who figured out where she was going and how to call the house. Didn't even bite at her offer to run off together. He came wanting all the money. He would have gotten it too, if Ramon hadn't've finally shown back up.

Though all of that made enough sense to Ramon, one thing was off: Why was Shelley pointing a gun at him? He'd done everything he said he would and he'd come back, like he promised. No words could form though. He stood looking at her, dumbfounded.

Shelley's smile made Ramon shiver inside, and her quick-on-her-feet explanation dropped the temperature even further. Sure, the plan was to divide the take and go their separate ways, but this dead guy and this big mess just changed all of that. She had no plans to kill Ramon because she didn't want a corpse in a house with her name on it, but now, look. By her estimation, two bodies were better than one. She'd leave one good bag of money, so that if and when any cops finally showed up, they'd figure these two thieves got in a row over their stolen goods. Shot each other. The Mexican one got the white guy pretty good, but he also got shot in the moment and bled out. Before Ramon could talk his way out of it, BLAM.

She put a bullet in his gut and he was on the floor, seeing stars. You really do see stars, he thought, as the pain overtook him with such force that he stopped thinking at all.

The world stopped turning. Air stood still. Ramon looked out the window, hoping for some sign that everything wasn't over. He could see the Santa Rosas reflected in the dining room mirror in one direction and the San Jacintos clouded in, up on high through the clerestories. Rectangular glass, around the top of the living room. Clerestories. He didn't know that word before Shelley taught it to him.

He watched her walking away toward the dining area and noticed her outfit. A bright floral floor-length caftan. Yellow and orange. A slit went up one side revealing gold sandals, reminding him of a pair his mother Jilda stole and wore all one long summer, when he was a teen. She never owned any caftans, though. Shelley's mannish features reminded him of his mother even further.

My mother, Ramon thought, and likely even said it out loud: *Madre mia.* To Shelley it sounded like a normal exclamation you might make after such an event. Ramon blinked and wondered: Why would I be thinking about her? Like the wounded mind does, it danced, and he saw Jilda before him now, a ghost, proud that he would shoot so straight, like she taught him. Disappointed that he dropped the gun, she spoke or maybe he heard words without sound, but apparently she was here to teach him one last lesson. He belonged to her now, she said, a captive of their bloodline. Everyone who had died on this land also began to rise from the floor. They lifted Ramon up, levitating him closer to the mountain views.

He wanted nothing other than to see Babe. No money. No cars. Nothing. Just Babe. His mother morphed into Howie Mandel, as can happen in a moment of dreamy delirium, and Ramon used the very last of his strength to slam down a red button that, in reality, was not there. "Deal!" he yelled, as his body fell crashing down from the ceiling.

Shelley looked over at him as he lost consciousness and slumped.

TWENTY-FOUR

The first sound of gunfire worried Babe, because it meant something went wrong enough that Ramon had to shoot her to get out alive. But the second one sent him into a panic. Were they both dead? Was he wrong for not running in to find out? From his vantage point all he could make out was the blue front door of the house. Houses in Kings Point had to be white, but apparently you could paint your doors to express some kind of personality. Shelley's were a bright blue, but not royal or aqua. He could only describe it as Yves Klein blue. Deep, dark, mysterious, impossible to define. He used to utilize Klein Blue to teach because the artist described it as an "open window to freedom, as the possibility of being immersed in the immeasurable existence of color." That's what he believed good singing was: not tone, per se, but immersion, purity.

When Shelley pushed two duffle bags through the blue doors and out on to the covered entry, his confusion ran even higher. He assumed it was all she could carry, two bags at a time, and after closing the door behind her, she hobbled roughly down the street, around the corner and behind the bushes to where the Rolls had been stashed. She hustled back quickly, shut the door behind her, and then re-emerged, repeating the task.

Babe knew there were eight bags total, so he figured she'd be in and out four times. After that second exit and return, he brought himself as close to the side of the house as he could without being seen. When she got half way down the road, he stole himself quickly inside and almost lost it when he saw all that blood.

Ramon was lying in a growing red puddle, breathing heavily, but otherwise inert. His weapon sat on the floor where he dropped it, a good arm's length out of reach. One bag was by the door, the other between the two splayed bodies. Nothing make sense to him, but it didn't matter. The sound of the Rolls pulling up was followed by the clicking of Shelley's heels approaching the door. He grabbed Ramon's pistol, braced himself behind the silver circular sofa, and let Shelley get fully back inside before he shot her dead. A lot. Not just with one bullet. With everything left in the gun. He didn't want to be talked out of it or fooled any further. This needed to end, and he was making sure it was over. But unlike Shelley, at this point, Babe had no plan at all.

Now the two bags of money drew a line between Shelley and the other dead guy. The motor of the Rolls was running and six out of eight duffle bags were in the trunk.

You never know how you will behave in a moment of sheer terror and crisis, but to Babe's surprise, he felt clear. Focused even, and aware of the simple truths. Five loud gun shots had been fired. Two people were dead, and two things became obvious to him: one, he needed to get out of there and two, he wasn't leaving alone.

As easy as it was to toss Ramon around in bed, it was near impossible to move him now. He dragged Ramon towards the foyer, and luckily, the way Shelley fell after the impact of the bullets landed her over to the side enough to get the door open. Gruesome was the only way to describe the scene, but Babe knew he had no time to waste.

Ramon came awake enough so as to get his arm up around Babe's shoulders, and to help him hobble to the roomy back seat. The good fortune continued: not only had the rain resumed, sprinkling hard enough to wash away the few signs of the body being dragged to the car, but Shelley's interior seats were dark brown leather so blood wasn't showing as much as if they were, say, that creamy white-beige you've seen inside these cars on TV.

His wits still with him, Babe decided he had to go in the house one more time—to shower the crimson off his forearms and neck, to get a change of clothes, to grab some blankets to cover Ramon. And a hat. He needed Ramon's cowboy hat, to put over his eyes, so when they crossed the border, he'd just look like he was sleeping. Who knows how long all of that would take, and if he had the stomach to pull it off.

This he did know: showering carried him back to his first moment here, only this time, he had no gumption to answer any questions about his feelings. Instead, he scrubbed himself, hard, and watched blood, Ramon's blood, swirl around the drain and disappear. He let the water run over him, red hot, trying to jumpstart his skin. He dried himself with something, it must have been a towel. He dressed, a plain black t-shirt and jeans. Nothing to stand out. He gathered what he remembered to gather. Plus a bottle of booze. He needed that for later.

Just before he made his exit, he lost his breath. Or maybe his heart skipped a beat. Momentum fell away. He was standing there, in the foyer, directionless for that long moment, staring at one of those John Baldessari dot artworks where the identity of the three people in the photo had been obliterated by big circles of primary colors. It was clear the door's hue had been color-matched to one of the dots, so it wasn't Klein Blue after all, it was Baldessari Blue.

TWENTY-FIVE

Babe sat behind the wheel of an insanely conspicuous stolen car with an undocumented gay Mexican hustler in the back seat, bleeding to death from a bullet wound to the gut, and close to two million illicitly obtained American dollars in the trunk. He was pointed towards the border and driving the speed limit.

Crossing into Mexico is not as easy as you might think but of course Shelley had thought all of that out for them. The fastest and least conspicuous way to get safely over the border is by route of the Salton Sea and then on to the essentially lawless border of Mexicali. Shelley assumed that Ramon would be solo so she strongly suggested he go that way, and then figured he'd disappear deeper into the country. Ramon, though, made it clear he wanted to go home.

The trip to Playas de Tijuana might be more direct from Palm Springs if you pass through San Diego and enter at San Ysidro, and fuck all if Babe was not going to grant his dying wish, but still he thought better of trying to get through a major metropolis. They'd go the route Shelley prescribed and then make the extra two-hour drive inside of Mexico, back to the coast line.

Passing the Salton Sea, he needed a bathroom break, but there's nothing there. The whole thing is a monument to human failure, created by incompetence a hundred-plus years ago when a plan to subvert water from the Colorado River for farming went haywire and flooded the area for two full years until it could be contained. Sometime in the 1950s developers saw that big body of water and decided to try making a resort out of it—water skiing, bathing beauties, the works—which naturally became a whole new disaster by the 1970s when the lake started to shrink, farmers dumped contaminants into it, and the fresh water transformed to saline making temperatures in the lake rise so high that fish died *en masse*, blighting the beaches of the sea with their carcasses. What looked and smelled like kind of a seafood holocaust destroyed the tourism, surprise surprise, and now all that's left a half century later are the footprints of hotel rooms and tennis courts and empty pools, and some comic real estate signs offering lots for sale to build your waterside dream house. The odor also remains, and on bad windy days, the sulfur stink wafts all the way across the Coachella Valley. Sonny Bono, one-time mayor of Palm Springs after his own career dried up when Cher left him, had plans for an overhaul and revival that were interrupted when he ran afoul of a tree in a skiing accident and died, extending the curse for at least another generation.

Babe held his nose and tried not to gag as he relieved himself at the sea's edge, littered with broken beer bottles and fast food wrappers left by the new generation of tourists who come just to cluck their tongues at the incredible waste of opportunity. The American Dream, exposed to be the house of cards it is.

Babe moved papers he'd need at the crossing, out of the glove box and up on the dash. He wanted his U.S. passport at the ready and there was already a temporary import permit Shelley arranged so this car was able to move freely beyond the border zones, assuming it wasn't seized the minute he showed his ID, or Ramon's expired Mexican passport. Don't borrow trouble from tomorrow, he thought. For now, just drive.

There was no need to slap himself to stay awake tonight. His senses were alert. Too alert, so he tried to distract himself by staring at the lines in the road. He watched the razor sharp edge of the hood race past the yellow dashes. It was interrupted only by the white lines of the tires of trucks beside him, going round on the oily wet hot pavement. Steel, hurtling forward, away. In front of him, another line, the horizon. This is what he tried to focus on. Not what happened today, or any of the days preceding.

Considering all that had gone sideways and still

could go upside down, he found he was able to calm himself this way, surprisingly unrattled. The silence got to him after a while, so he turned on the stereo, and a favorite rarity made famous by Donna Loren was winding up to the big finish—and yes, he sang along:

So please don't worry if I sigh for him

You know that I'll get by

I'll just pretend that it's not the end;
    it only hurts when I cry

He appreciated the way Ms. Loren sang the chorus, amping it up another level with each repeat, until the final crescendo:

It only hurts when I cry

It only hurts when I cry

It only hurts when I cry

This is one he did not think he could do better on. Her vocal was perfect. In fact, if he were to do a concert, and he decided to sing this song, he'd introduce it by saying she sang it first and best, and he could only hope he did it justice.

He turned on the car heat. He felt cold and exposed, like that moment right after sex when your lover is wanting an intimacy your body refuses to return. You avert your eyes. You lob in an inappropriate off-color joke. You do anything to keep from feeling what you are really feeling which is scared to death that someone will finally see inside of you, and not want what is there.

Lines again, this time in the sky. Telephone poles. Connecting calls, from this person to that person. Fathers and sons no longer estranged, lovers separated but able to coo, business being negotiated, best friends catching up. Banalities. Life changing moments. He looked around him, at the few cars on the road at this hour, mostly single people looking straight ahead, going who knows where for who knows what reason. Driving to get there, wherever there is.

As if the Salton Sea was gurgling back up in the back of his throat, he felt like he might throw up, so he pulled over at what promised to be the last rest stop before the border. He parked way over to the side so no one would see and took the opportunity to redress Ramon's wounds. The more casually they behaved, he decided, the less anyone would give them notice, and it was true. He fake-yawned for whatever audience he might have, stretched his limbs, and bought bottled water at the vending machine.

No one blinked when he went from the backseat to the overflowing garbage can like many a traveler before him, but then who would guess he was discarding clothes soaked with blood. He lifted someone else's hefty bag to hide his under it, and that worked out just fine. Being a criminal is odd, he thought, because you find yourself coming up with all sorts of solutions to solve problems you never thought yourself capable of overcoming, or having.

Careful not to get any blood on himself, he petted Ramon's brow and warned it was going to hurt when he poured booze on the wound. Ramon would have to do his best not to yell out, but you know, everyone has seen that in the movies, so Babe was pretty certain it was a good idea. Plus, it was going to make Ramon smell of liquor when they had to get by the border patrol, and that was part of the scenario he planned on painting. My friend in the back seat, he would say, is asleep and fighting off a pretty good hangover. All he needed Ramon to do, he told him, was open his eyes and moan a little, and speak some slurry Spanish.

All Babe needed Ramon to do was not die on him.

Coming into Mexico, the line up of cars, whether massive or a smattering, gets assaulted by vendors selling everything from Donald Trump piñatas to "deluxe" pearl rosaries on "real" silver chains, so it's a slow crawl. Still, if for some reason you do not want to cross from the US to Mexicali, you actually have to be careful not to make the wrong turn and get funneled through fast, with no way to U-turn around. They clearly want us in Mexico. We get drunk, and eat in restaurants, we buy knock-off goods, and, bottom-line, spend money. What we don't do is respect their culture so it's no surprise we just look like big and fat and stupid dollar signs to them.

The border guy was about to wave him on through when he noticed Ramon's passport was expired. There's a place you have to go line up to renew it, but he didn't think the *borracho* would survive the hour-plus wait, so they might just have to be taken aside to talk with his boss. He flashed a big gold-toothed smile as he handed the passport book back to Babe, who got the message, slid two $100 bills into its pages, and handed it back, asking him to check the date again. Slam, down went the metal stamp on the back page of Ramon's passport, and they were through.

See, that's the trouble with the world, Ramon told him, weakly from the back. "Them that's got shall get," answered Babe, "and them that's not shall lose. So the bible says, and it still is news." Ramon laughed, and the two men clasped hands over the seat.

They stayed that way until they reached the ocean, where Babe had to pry Ramon's cold fingers loose from his own so he could get out of the car.

TWENTY-SIX

The dirty-white beach at Playas de Tijuana stretches right up to the border. Family members on the other side meet their relatives through the fence, passing notes and cards with credit on them for Costco and Amazon and iTunes. This is the hour they prefer, the deadmost part of the morning's night which comes before sunrise, when just one lazy gunman stands on a rock, an indifferent guard, still hours before the full-on persecution of the dividing line gets awakened. This time-void is when the tide ebbs low and they can actually hug, knee deep in the water, beyond the barb-wire topped chain link fence. It's that easy to cross, but, on the other side, what would you do to survive? You become a fugitive without papers. You live in the shadows, like a shadow. Here, people have jobs and extended family and their homes. They have recipes they like to make, and a language they can speak to each other.

Away from these townspeople, Babe stood alone on the rough rugged sand, watching waves go in and out. The long line of spray, the grating roar against the pebbles, the tremulous cadence, an eternal note of sadness, the turbid ebb and flow...and the rest of that verse he once had to memorize, so long ago in school. This was poetry writ large as the sun began to rise behind him, up over the hills and the city, turning the sky burnt orange, staining the blue black water. He could almost hear a sizzle as the starfire was released onto the tips of the surf. Laughing gulls hovered over the shallow foam, diving periodically to scoop up easy prey. He stood watching them, working together as a pack, as they'd eat live or dead things that washed up on the shore and harass other birds that found discarded human food.

He ran quickly through his life and confirmed: he'd never seen a person die before he shot Shelley. Outside of a few cuts and other run-ins with teenage injuries, he'd never seen much blood either, man or animal.

The gulls scavenged. Tides swirled. And try as he might, he simply could not piece everything together. Facts were missing. Moments were blurred. Ramon lay stiffening on the seat. Only it wasn't Ramon anymore. Shelley's money was in the trunk. Only it never was her money.

Looking around, the morning light revealed faces where before there had only been silhouettes. Babe recognized he was the foreigner now. Refusing other, harder, harsher thoughts, he dropped his head and decided he would need to learn more Spanish.

"¿Le gustaría un perro, señor?"

Babe raised his eyes to see a young street kid, black hair and green eyes, holding a baby white pitbull.

"What's its name?" he asked. The kid shrugged.

"Como quiere." Whatever you want.

"How about Daisy?" but even the boy knew that was a girl's name and this puppy was a boy. He turned the dog over and showed him, "Oopsy, mister."

"Oopsy daisy," said Babe.

And the dog barked. He seemed to like that name.

"How much? ¿Cuánto cuesta?"

"Como quiere." Whatever you want.

He had half a mind to give the kid a whole duffle bag full. Hell, maybe he should just give the trunk load to him. But Babe was awake and aware enough to grasp that he couldn't just walk away and leave the money. He'd need it to survive. Anyway, he knew it'd rain nothing but trouble down upon the kid and his whole family, or anyone else who happened upon it, for that matter. More practicalities flashed: He needed to get rid of the car. And Ramon's body. That thought alone was enough to make him cry.

The kid was still standing there, with the puppy.

Babe clicked open the trunk with the remote control key, and peeled a $100 off a stack. The kid's eyes lit up when he held it out. What a score! He dumped the puppy into Babe's arms and ran before the dumb American could change his mind. Babe looked Oopsydaisy in the eye, and, realizing how permanently his fate had changed, sang to him:

Ninety-nine miles from L.A...

His voice cracked, unstable, unable to sustain notes to continue the serenade, but he did not let himself fall apart. He got into the car without looking into the backseat, because after singing "their" song, that would surely break his heart.

He put the mutt on his lap and started up the engine. Oopsydaisy was happy as a clam at high tide, curling up on his new owner, safe for the time being from predators and the insensitive outside world he'd only moments ago escaped.

Babe steered the car across the street to the parking area of a small empty church he had passed on his way to the shore lot. He kissed Ramon's lips. His wrist. Everything, cold. It took all his strength, of heart and core, to get Ramon out of the back seat and onto the steps of the mission.

One last look out at the ocean.

And Babe was gone.

ACKNOWLEDGMENTS

Words can't express the gratitude I feel towards my husband and creative partner Todd Hughes who for thirty years has seen in me what no one else in the world sees. He read the roughest early draft of this book as well as the final polished version and cried all through it both times because he is likely the only person who knows which parts I made up and which parts I did not.

Hat tips are due to my first and second draft responders/readers, Eileen Jones and Shannon Metcalf, who said yes to the dreadful ask from a friend to read something unfinished in order to help it get over the finish line. Joan Gand offered to "read for typos" and must be thanked for that thankless task, especially since she found some, so apologies to The Gaffe Squad who hopefully now have nothing to do. A special acknowledgment goes to Donna Loren, who took us to see a Johnny Mathis concert, on her birthday, as it is the first time I heard the song that is the title of this book, and that fateful event set my imagination in motion.

I owe a certain amount of inspiration to the places where I did the bulk of the writing, home in Palm Springs, and on retreat in Provincetown and up in the high desert near Joshua Tree.

Finally, Mark Givens deserves accolades for his elegant and thoughtful editing, as I now get credit for his restraint and good taste.

A word must be said about Killer, our first lady pit bull, who really did spend her last hour in the UCLA sculpture garden, and Butchie, who followed in her paw prints, as the character of Daisy is based on them both. Our current girls, Fido Galore and Oopsydaisy spent many an hour at my feet while I wrote, and listened to me work out story issues with Todd while on our walks.

Not only do the Ebersole Hughes dogs all get a shout out for that essential assist, but a portion of the proceeds from each sale of this book will be donated to benefit the Palm Springs Animal Shelter, a no-kill facility whose mission statement, in part, says that every animal deserves a loving, safe, healthy environment in which they can thrive. For more information, please visit https://psanimalshelter.org/

ABOUT THE AUTHOR

P. David Ebersole is an American television director and independent filmmaker, working in both narrative and documentary. Born and raised in Hollywood, he is the son of a psychologist and his stepfather was the City Editor of the Los Angeles Times.

He began his film career as a child actor, playing the lead in the musical *Junior High School* (1978), which also co-starred Paula Abdul. Stepping behind the camera, he earned his MFA winning AFI's Franklin J. Schaffner award for best film/best director for his student thesis project, *Death in Venice, Ca* (1994).

He directed the boxing film *Straight Right* (2000) and two prime time telenovelas, *Desire* (2006) and *Wicked Wicked Games* (2007) starring Tatum O'Neal. He was co-producer of the HBO original film, *Stranger Inside* (2001) and the independent film *The New Women* (2001) starring Mary Woronov.

He directed and edited his first theatrically released documentary *Hit So Hard* (2012) about drummer Patty Schemel of the seminal grunge band Hole. Along with his husband and business partner Todd Hughes, he is Executive Producer of the subjective documentary *Room 237* (2012), and *Dear Mom,*

Love Cher (2013), which he also directed. The duo co-directed and produced *Mansfield 66/67* (2017) about the last two years of Jayne Mansfield's life, the award-winning *House of Cardin* (2019), and *My Name Is Lopez* (2021) about trailblazing Latino rock and roller Trini Lopez.

He lives in Palm Springs with his husband and two lady pit bull rescues, Fido Galore and Oopsydaisy.

This is his first novel.

PALM SPRINGS ANIMAL SHELTER
www.psanimalshelter.org

the
ebersole
hughes
company

www.ebersolehughes.com
info@ebersolehughes.com

112 Harvard Ave #65

Claremont, CA 91711 USA

pelekinesis@gmail.com

www.pelekinesis.com

Pelekinesis titles are available through Small Press Distribution, Baker & Taylor, Ingram, Bertrams, and directly from the publisher's website.

CPSIA information can be obtained
at www.ICGtesting.com
Printed in the USA
BVHW032207160422
634530BV00005B/199